S0-BYQ-410

Bugging In

To Deborah,

Get Busy.

Cheers

Joe Smith

Bugging In:

A Novel of Societal Collapse

Joe Snuffy

CreateSpace

Copyright (c) 2017. First Edition. All rights reserved. Any unauthorized duplication of any portion of this book in any form will be prosecuted to the fullest extent of the law.

CreateSpace.

Fiction

Second Printing

First Printing December, 2016

Editing: Anonymous, J. Snuffy

ISBN-13: 978-1977517142

ISBN-10: 1977517145

All rights reserved. Any unauthorized duplication in whole or in part or dissemination of this novel by any means will be prosecuted to the fullest extent of the law. This book is a work of fiction. All of the characters and events portrayed in this book are fictitious. The author shall have neither liability nor responsibility to any citizen, person, or entity with respect to any loss or damage caused, or alleged to be caused, directly or indirectly, by the information contained in this novel. Any resemblances to living people (other than felines) is purely coincidental.

DEDICATION

To my grandson Logan, and to the rest of his generation.
Hopefully they will form a more self-reliant and ethical culture as
they survive the collapse of industrialized civilization, this century.

It was actually pleasant for an early March winter morning. Lying in bed Paul could see the daylight through the blinds, although the window faced west and the sun was rising on the other side of the house. He could see the birds, but not hear them through the heavily insulated house with white vinyl argon gas-filled windows. His wife, Emily had already left for work.

He felt good having run long and hard the previous day. He would run again today, but not as far. His large, light-brown and black tiger-striped cat, resembling a bobcat was there on the blankets, curled-up next to him on the queen-sized bed.

"Hi Tiny Baby," he said to her. Paul had gotten her as a kitten from the Humane Society. In her display cage she had been incredibly playful and charming, as she observed the crowd of people on the morning of Adoption Saturday. After bringing her home he kept calling her Tiny Baby, or Tiny Baby Kitty. Eventually, the name stuck. She was now a large cat, fully-grown. A big little child, Paul liked to think of her as he took into account that cats age roughly five years for every one human year. At about one-and-a-half years old, Paul figured she was about eight years-old in cat years.

Paul gave Tiny Baby a kiss on her forehead as he got out of bed, dressed in a matching pair of brown briefs and T-shirt. He liked the older-generation military issue colors. After putting on a pair of black athletic shorts, Paul went into the kitchen in order to morning hydrate; getting some water into him while making some coffee.

Paul was 51, and in better physical shape than most twenty-somethings. You had to be in shape if you were going to survive the collapse of industrialized civilization, he used to jokingly tell his friends. Paul was 200 pounds-even, brown/gray-haired, brown eyes, with large front thigh muscles. Those had come from years of running, military road marches, running with a backpack, etc.

With his coffee in hand he went online in his living room with his netbook. Checking RT.com, he saw the usual white propaganda. White propaganda. The same stuff the Allies used on Germany and Japan during WWII, because we were the good guys and we didn't have to lie. Now it was the other way around. *Russia Today* was Russian state-funded, and gave truthful propaganda a whole new meaning. It was one of the best progressive news sources out there for real information, as compared to the heavily doctored and trivial US media, which was desperately continuing to force-feed the American public with a false image of carefree and abundant life within the U.S.

Paul grabbed the remote for the large flat-panel TV in his living room. Since it was early enough, out of morbid curiosity he flipped through channels, looking for some network news. He landed on ABC's *Good Morning America*. Instead of news or information there was a football game-type stage setting, with a mock-up of a mini-football field. There were some people dressed as referees, with pairs of brides and grooms, all in full dress.

My God, Paul thought. This feel-good propaganda about life in

America was going to continue right up until the very end, Paul knew: just as the preaching of military victory did in Germany and Japan, until their ends came in 1945. In the meantime, people would delve even deeper into their NFL/NASCAR/Disneyland worlds until the next job loss, or the next bout of homelessness, at least. Then they would just kill themselves, and maybe even someone else as their cognitive dissonance, and dashed economic expectations became unbearable. The mass shootings were now occurring several times *a day* within the US, after all.

America, the indispensable nation, the light on the hill. What a laugh, Paul thought. Many disconnected people in Washington actually believed this; that the world could not *do without* the U.S. This had been an imperial delusion going back at least as far as the Romans, who spouted the same crap, even as their own empire was well into decline. If anything the world had been siding with Russia and China, because of all of the eavesdropping, political interference, the military interventions, etc., of the U.S. Government. Sovereign countries around the world were getting tired of being told what to do and how to do it, by the U.S.

Snuffy

* * *

Gregory Durham, an elderly gray-haired senator who looked like his barber regularly used a chainsaw on him, sat at his dimly-lit desk, looking out of the window of his dark-oak-paneled senatorial office in Washington DC. He had a small glass in his hand with some Johnny Walker Black poured into it. He had stayed late on a dark, snowy, wintery early evening, wanting to be by himself. That's funny, he thought: He should be drinking Johnny Walker Red, since he was from a red state. He was starting to feel good now.

Wait a minute: When he had been a younger politician, "red" had meant being a communist. Whatever. Who the hell came up with that red state / blue state crap anyway? Just another example of how stupid the American public were, he thought to himself. He sat looking at the snow-surrounded U.S. capitol building, with its beefed-up perimeter of Jersey barriers, rolls of military concertina wire, roving US Army troops in their Extreme Cold Weather System uniforms and large floodlights.

The people hate us? Good. Whatever. For years he had supported everything that the public had hated: The USA PATRIOT Act, the wars in Iraq and Afghanistan, the NSA surveillance, military action against Russia over Ukraine and Syria, etc. He only answered to the interests of the people who mattered for both he and his family: The so-called military-industrial complex and the CEO's who ran the respective aerospace and defense companies. The stupid-ass public didn't even know what that meant, much less that Eisenhower's outgoing presidential speech had originally referred to a military-industrial-congressional complex, prior to the word 'congressional' being removed at the last minute by his speechwriters.

Senator Durham had traveled overseas visiting the troops, embassies, etc. over the years, and was not impressed by the average people in the Middle East, in particular. And people thought Americans were stupid. In some of these countries, whether Iraq, Afghanistan, or elsewhere, they were outright retarded. A bunch of mentally arrested fucks. The U.S. was the indispensable nation, after all with smarter people running it than anywhere else. There were some, like that one Government Accounting Office director who had said years ago that we were following in the footsteps of the Roman Empire. That was just horseshit. This is the new history. *Our* history.

That's all right, he continued thinking to himself. The people don't like us? Don't like *me* anymore? That's OK. I've got something for them. Being a member of the Senate Armed Services Committee, he knew people at the Council on Foreign Relations and at the Pentagon who felt just like he did. He smiled as his thoughts were going through his mind. Looking into the darkness through the window of his dimly-lit office, he picked up his secure cell phone, hit a pre-dialed number and put it to his ear. He and his family would be safe over the state line in Pennsylvania, at any event.

"Military Command Center Watch Officer. Can I help you?"
"This is Senator Durham. I need your boss on the phone, now..."

* * *

Paul was having the perfect morning at the end of the leather couch in their living room: a fresh cup of brewed coffee, his netbook computer, and Tiny Baby, facing away, sitting like a sphinx on Paul's crossed legs, his sweatpants and thick socks resting on the coffee table. He was looking at some stock charts of his favorite exchange-traded funds. He then commenced to do some writing.

Suddenly, Paul heard the doorbell ring. Ding dong. What the hell, he thought. It was around 9:30 in the morning. He walked towards the front door. Wait a second: I must not have had enough coffee this morning. Instead, he went into his wife's office, the window being next to the front door. He moved the closed white mini-blinds just a tiny bit, and could see someone with a clipboard: a skinny twenty-something, who looked as innocent as someone out of a Norman Rockwell print.

Uh uh. I'm not opening the door for this little clown, Paul thought. As he watched, the kid rang the doorbell a second time. The kid waited. He then looked back towards the street where an old white Nissan sedan was parked, with two other males in the front seats. The kid then opened the glass-and-metal storm door. He tried the doorknob of the white steel door, which had an extra brass-looking steel strike plate reinforcing the doorknob and deadbolt.

Paul quickly ran for the safe in his study, a tall twenty-gun black gun safe. A series of electronic beeps as he keyed in the combo, then a solid steel *ca-clunk* sound as he opened the door, and pulled out a Springfield Armory XD pistol, in .45 ACP. It was soft-edge DuraCoat painted in a combination of OD green, coyote and CADPAT Light Green. Looking out of his own window facing the street, he saw the person who had been at the door, now back at the car, talking to the occupants inside. The kid got into the back seat, while another male with darker features got out of the front passenger side, heading towards the north side of his house. I guess they're not going to try the steel front door, Paul thought.

Suddenly he heard a three-part electronic warble alert from the monitor in front of him, below the window in his study. It was a six-inch wireless monitor, receiving signal from the LOREX camera on the north side of his house where his flat-coyote painted 1990 Dodge Diesel pickup was parked. He noticed the person who had come out of the vehicle on the monitor, as he approached the gate in the six-foot wooden fence. He looked like a tall, skinny teen or twenty-something, wearing one of those ghetto-wannabe hats with the bill facing backward. The angled camera caught the kid as he approached the walkway between the truck and the house. Paul put his Danner tactical boots on quickly, just making one big knot at the top of each boot. At least he had socks on. His gray sweatpants made the ensemble look goofy.

Paul ran into the back dining room, then slipped through the sliding glass doors, into the back yard and towards the locked gate. There was a blue food-grade rain catchment barrel at that corner of the house. Paul knelt down next to it, as the kid blindly fiddled with the padlocked latch that he couldn't see on Paul's side of the wooden gate.

As the burglar continued fiddling, Paul thought of something. As lazy as these punks are, they also appeared unarmed. He set the .45 XD down and buried it in some old bark dust, then reached for his keys in the waistband of his shorts. He found the padlock key.

As quickly as the burglar quit the padlocked latch, Paul got up from his crouch, quietly unlocked the padlock, threw open the gate, and ran after the guy. The noise from opening the gate alarmed the little goofy hat-wearing ghetto wannabe, who saw Paul just a few steps behind him. As the burglar started his sprint, his buddies in the beat up-looking white Nissan took off, abandoning him.

As Paul lived on the corner of an intersection, he chased the little punk across the street, next to Paul's neighbors' house, which faced his own. Paul closed in on him, as they were sprinting down the street. Paul's right boot went up, like a football player's kick-off. Wham! A snap-kick to the punk's groin from behind. The kick practically picked the kid up into the air, before he fell on his face. Some vomit came out of the kid's mouth. Paul stumbled and fell onto the pavement himself, rolling off of his shoulders.

"Ow," Paul groaned, laying on the ground, on his stomach. He was too old to be tumbling on pavement, like this. Thank God he stayed in shape as much as he did. He saw the kid, also laying in the street, behind him.

Paul slowly got up and walked back to the kid, giving him a kick in the head, in a glancing blow. It wasn't hard enough to kill him or knock him unconscious, but the kid definitely felt it. The teen or twenty-something had a whitewall-style haircut, and a gold chain around his neck. Paul grabbed him by it. It broke. He then grabbed him by his shirt. Paul saw the car with the other criminals in it, about 70 yards away, stopping at the next intersection, to see what happened to their buddy. Paul pulled the punk up to his knees, and yelled out to the car.

"Hey, does this piece of shit belong to you?"

The two occupants looked straight at Paul and their buddy for a moment, then took-off quickly, again. Paul then pushed the punk into the street, where he fell again.

"What are you trying to do, break into my house, you stupid little fuck?" Paul yelled his question at him. He then grabbed the punk by his shirt, with both hands.

"Uh...uh...no."

"Yeah you did, you stupid little fuck!"

At that moment, Paul punched him in the head, with his right. He left him lying there, and walked home.

* * *

Senator Durham and each of the United States military's four Chiefs of Staff, each in the dress uniform of their respective service, sat at a white circular table inside of a secure room, deep underground, within the Pentagon. Its circular white-colored walls and vaulted ceiling resembled the inside of a spacecraft. Each of them had one or two assistants, sitting with them. A faint electrical hum could be heard in the background.

"We already know that the Chinese have been conducting training exercises, simulating an invasion of Japan," the Army Chief of Staff told the senator.

"How many troops are we talking about here?" the senator asked.

The Army Chief of Staff's J-2 (Intelligence Officer), another general officer, spoke up:

"It looks to us like they're planning to task their entire active military. The People's Revolutionary Army alone has about 2.3 million active duty, not counting an 800,000-man reserve. An actual draft is the scary part. They have over 600 million adults who are considered fit for military service, along with another 20 million entering conscription age each year. Open source intel also indicates that there is currently a huge anti-Japanese sentiment, throughout the Chinese populace."

The Senator's face got red. "Holy shit! We know the Japanese are re-militarizing. We're even helping build-up Vietnam's military, if you can believe *that* shit. But all that doesn't mean anything. And we've only got an entire active and reserve military of just under three million, total. Great."

"You're essentially correct, Senator," the intelligence officer replied. "In addition, the Japanese population is in steep decline, with an elderly demographic majority."

"That means we'll have to go nuclear anyway...uh, I mean nuclear, in order to keep our commitment to Japan."

"Pretty much," the Army Chief of Staff replied.

"Alright, I want everyone out of this room *now*, except for the

Chiefs," Senator Durham yelled, looking around the room.

A mix of Army, Air Force, Navy and Marine Corps semi dress uniforms began filing out of the room. Senator Durham watched until the last one, a Marine Colonel in his khaki's, left the room He then turned towards the four-star officers.

"Alright, we've talked about this shit before. We know things are getting bad, with this debt crisis, the drought out in the west, the hurricanes, and all the other shit going on in this country. And all those shale oil plays here in The States fell on their face as soon as they started. Why the fuck didn't anybody mention the fact that they weren't even making money from the drilling, just bullshit loans from Wall Street," the senator yelled his question at the Joint Chiefs. The four senior military officers simply looked back at him, with blank looks on their faces.

"Half of the states in the U.S. are now calling for secession, for Christ's sake," the senator added. He put his head in his hands for a moment, then, looking up, continued his tirade.

"And the Chinese, those motherfuckers. They just declared their own reserve currency, and backed by all of that gold they've been buying over the years. We've been entertaining this shit for far too long. They've been playing our asses long enough, not to mention starting that AIIB bank of theirs, back in 2014, to replace our IMF and World Bank, in Asia. And when we wanted a piece of that action, those motherfuckers just gave us the finger! They literally laughed at us! Besides, the CFR made that one report public, back in early 2015, saying that we needed to take China out. I say we release the nukes, and do the strategic strike on the Chinese, that we've already been talking about. That should take their asses out. We've got a shitload of ABM capability surrounding both China and Russia, for Christ's sake. Am I wrong?"

The Joint chiefs simply sat there, shaking their heads, slightly.

"We need to stay clear of Russia," the Army Chief of Staff told the group. "We need to let them know if we can that we don't want a fight with them. Ever since Syria they've been demonstrating capabilities and technologies that we don't even have any countermeasures for. And since NATO practically no longer exists, we sure as hell don't want a fight with them."

"Yeah, fucking Russians," Senator Durham said, looking down at the table. "If any Chinese nukes do get through and hit the US, they'll probably just take out the troublemakers here anyway. That's what we're hoping for, anyway, right? We could wipe China off the map, as of fucking yesterday, without even thinking about it."

"We would need someone to obtain the football from the guy who's currently assigned," the US Marine Corps Chief replied. He was referring to the senior officer who accompanies the President of the United States, with a 45-pound briefcase, steel-cabled to his wrist, which holds the authentication codes and SATCOM radio, in order for the President of the United States to authorize a strategic nuclear strike.

"Yeah, and which of us is 'gonna be the President and Vice President, especially for re-verification," the Army Chief replied?

"We'll authorize it ourselves. The President and his staff have been taken out, leaving us to authorize the strike, The Air Force Chief replied. I just haven't thought-up the rest. The good news is that the rest of the CFR is on board, and likes your idea, Senator."

"So they're somehow neutralized and we get all of the launch authentications?" Senator Durham asked.

"That could be done. Through some good old compartmentalization at J-SOC, we get some of their people to do it, just like the same people who planted the thermite charges in the World Trade Center buildings about a week before 9/11," the Navy Chief of Staff replied.

"Yeah, except they fucked-up and brought a third building down that hadn't even been touched by *anything*," the Air Force four-star noted. "Besides, there's still video out there, showing the charges detonating, as the buildings imploded, for Christ's sake."

"Or, you mean like the ones who messed with that journalist Hastings' Mercedes, back in 2013?" the Air Force four-star asked the group.

The Joint Chiefs all laughed.

The Navy Admiral spoke up again, interrupting the laughter: "We should be able to pull-off a compartmentalized 9/11-type operation, where if any part of it fails, we can tie it off and attribute it to lone terrorists, etcetera, etcetera."

Senator Durham spoke up. "OK, it looks like we're all on the same sheet of music here. I think we can get this ball rolling. If this works, then I'll be congratulating you guys after we all get settled-in at Site R."

* * *

The intelligence asset stood-by on a side street in downtown Washington DC wearing unassuming street clothes: blue jeans and a gray sweatshirt without any logos or any other distinguishing print-work. The only giveaway was a pair of tactical boots that simply appeared as outdoor shoes, underneath the jeans. He was not aware of anyone else involved in this operation and the actual identity of whom he was working for was kept classified. As soon as the Marine One helicopter lifted-off from the White House grounds, the former special operations soldier received an incoming ring on his smart phone. At that moment, he pulled a large rectangular-shaped cardboard box from his gray sedan, placing it on his right shoulder.

Concealed inside the cardboard box was an FIM-92 Stinger anti-aircraft missile system. The contractor aimed his Stinger at the President's helicopter. He achieved lock-on right away, as indicated by an electronic alarm sound which was muffled by a piece of OD green duct tape. As soon as he heard his smart phone ring a second time, BOOM! An initial charge kicked the missile out of its tube, as its rocket motor kicked-in.

Suddenly there were a total of four white missile trails now heading towards Marine One simultaneously, from locations surrounding the White House.

At the wreckage site a special Department of Defense team arrived, showed their credentials, then retrieved the nuclear football from the wrist of the dead military aide. In addition, they searched the pockets of both the President and Vice President, in the event that they had their individual authentication codes on their persons. All the other first responders were oblivious, as they operated from a state of shock. The DOD team left just as quickly as they had arrived. This was the actual drill to be performed after all, in the event of such a calamity.

* * *

"Yes, Senator Durham we have the football, and all the authentications," the Army Chief-of Staff told the Senator over their secure phone line.

"Great! I just sent an ultimatum to the Chinese but, they won't have time to respond to it anyway," the senator said, sitting in his senatorial office. Oh well. Launch 'em. I'm outa' here." he added.

With the news of Marine One being shot down, many congressmen, senators and other VIP's were retrieving their families and already heading to their designated civil defense shelters. Senator Durham would simply be part of that crowd.

Missile silos in the U.S., submarines in the Pacific Ocean and B-52 bombers were alerted and informed that this was not a drill. They were also sent updated target lists, indicating mainland China. They had already received news of the President and Vice President's deaths. They waited for their authentications from the Pentagon. As soon as the authentication codes matched, pairs of individuals sat or stood in front of their control panels, in land-based control rooms, and in submarines, out-to-sea. The missile officer in charge took a key from around his neck, opening the padlock, on a metal box. Out of the box, he grabbed two regular door knob-looking keys, and handed them out:

"Turn on my mark: Three, two, one, mark…"

* * *

Deep underground near Solnechnogorsk, Russia, was the command center of the Russian Air and Space Defense Forces. A Russian Air Force Colonel sat inside of a large box of forward-angled glass, looking out below at some large plasma screens in a darkened command and control facility. It was his shift as the senior watch officer. This was the Russian equivalent of the American's North American Aerospace Defense Command complex under Cheyenne Mountain, Colorado. Another officer approached the current senior watch officer. The entire command was already at a state of high-alert, based on intelligence coming out of the United States. Alarms were sounding within the complex.

"Well, what the fuck, Dmitri?"

"Sir, our early-warning satellites are giving us multiple missile launch indications coming out of the U.S. Based on their trajectory, their flight paths are taking them over Alaska and Eastern Siberia, into China. They'll be within range of our S-500 interceptors in about 15 minutes."

"I'm not aware of any war-footing between us and them. The mess over Syria was settled a long time ago. The U.S. tried to start a war with us, and they failed. We've had good relations with them ever since they stopped blaming us for their internal problems."

"Comrade Colonel, another duty officer yelled, as he stopped his run inside the glass office. We have nuclear detonations on the Chinese Coast!"

"What the fuck?" the Russian colonel yelled at his subordinates. "Are the Americans insane," he yelled to no one in particular.

A male civilian in a sharp-looking single-breast, gray Italian suite, white shirt with black tie, entered the office. Even without the sunglasses, he seemed to resemble one of the agents from the film *The Matrix*.

"Pavlov! What does the SVR have on this?"

"Nothing new to report, Comrade Colonel," the intelligence officer replied quickly. "We've been getting some chatter from within the U.S: A lot of internal conflict has been brewing. A possible coup attempt at the federal level, with mention of some sort of military action against China."

At that moment an older man, the Russian Air Force General in charge of the operation, dressed in a khaki semi-dress uniform entered the glass enclosure. "Those maniacs," the General replied. Suddenly an incoming video-teleconference was projected onto the glass in front of him. The Russian President and the rest of the Russian military general staff in separate video conference shots appeared at the bottom of the screen.

"Yes, Comrade President. We have incoming missiles from the US. The trajectories are taking them over Alaska and Eastern Siberia. However, we have no reported impacts within Russia. We are staying at Alert Condition One. All of the impacts appear to be happening in China."

One of the generals spoke up. "Very good, General. Maintain command and control of the facility. We will not counterattack unless a warhead detonates on Russian soil."

Yes, Comrade General.

The Russian President himself spoke up. "I want these missiles intercepted as soon as they reach Russian airspace. We have that capability, yes?"

The general in charge of the Russian Air Force, at the bottom of the video-teleconference image spoke up. "Mr. President, most of our missile interceptors are in the western half of the country, but we'll catch the ones that come into range."

* * *

As soon as nuclear detonations occurred on Chinese soil, the People's Revolutionary Army began launching their Dong Feng 41, or DF-41 intercontinental ballistic missiles. The existence of these extremely long-range, road-mobile ICBM's had not even been publicly acknowledged by the Chinese until 2014, in an internal state-sponsored propaganda piece. For some strange reason, within the same piece of propaganda, the Chinese had also named-off targets that they had intended to hit within the US. In addition to these new multiple independent re-entry vehicle (MIRV) missiles were other generations of short, intermediate and long-range nuclear missiles, such as the DF-5. All this, in addition to their submarine-launched nuclear missiles.

The first wave of intermediate and long-range missiles were armed with EMP-generating warheads, primarily intended as an electronic countermeasure, interfering with any missile interceptor systems, along with the desired secondary effects of wiping-out communications and power grids. These EMP devices were detonated over Guam, Hawaii, then Alaska, then Canada, as a wave of nuclear missiles came-in behind them. Although many Chinese missiles were intercepted in their boost phase, the defense systems of the United States were being overwhelmed.

Many of the missiles launched were mere decoys: The actual missiles, but with no live warheads. It was Sun Tzu at the strategic nuclear level. These missiles gave all the same thermal and radar signatures of any other missile carrying live independent warheads.

Multiple thermonuclear detonations occurred as air-bursts over Hawaii, the Seattle/Puget Sound area, San Diego, and San Antonio. These targets were prioritized due to their concentrated military presence. Other hits occurred over San Francisco and Los Angeles.

In the New England states, multiple targets were hit, to include New York, New Jersey, Baltimore, and Washington D.C. The

Chinese strategic intention was to focus on population centers, and by targeting the northeast of the United States, they knew they would eliminate a significant percentage of the U.S. population.

Luckily, many cities that would have served as secondary targets were spared due to military targeting priorities, missile intercepts, and missile malfunction. Many state capitals and "smaller" major cities such as Portland, Oregon were spared the direct effects of a nuclear strike.

However, the Chinese knew that they would not have to hit every major city within the U.S. in order to cause death and chaos, on a massive scale. Just removing transportation systems, the power grid, and many communications systems would suffice.

* * *

It was an overcast day, but not raining, at Paul's house. His wife, a software engineer was at work as usual. Another typical idyllic morning, in the life of an early-retired, financially independent individual, as he was typing-up the text for his next book: *Tactical Considerations for the Post-Collapse Environment*. He was getting really technically detailed here, as he worked on one of the chapters relating to camouflage. In this case, thermal and infrared (IR) signature management.

Tiny Baby was getting restless, jumping up into his lap, so he thought he'd take her out to the front yard with him. With his coffee in his left hand and the large bobcat-resembling female cat following him, Paul headed for the south side of his front yard. Here he grew his winter crops during the fall and winter, and potatoes during the spring and summer. Paul liked spending time with his crops. He likened it to when Einstein once described how solutions to complex problems simply came to him whenever he would take a walk in his garden. It also reminded him of how gardening was used as mental therapy. Paul had once seen something on TV about a program called Veterans to Farmers, where returning vets with PTSD were trained in large-scale organic agriculture, with stunning success. Beats the hell out of taking them out to a shooting range for therapy, he thought.

That thought reminded Paul of something else. Why did Clint Eastwood make such a propagandistic movie, years ago, about a famous sniper who outright lied about having killed people *within* the U.S., in addition to the total number he had killed in Iraq? All these falsehoods were contained within the ghost-written book that Eastwood had derived the movie from. Had he not noticed the questionable content? And within the context of an outright illegal invasion and occupation?

He knelt-down to check on the progress of this years' garlic crop, along with the Swiss chard and kale, the cool-weather greens they usually ate in their homegrown winter salads. These winter greens made some of the most naturally delicious salads he had ever eaten. The purple-colored kale was also unequaled as a leafy green for its nutritive content. Off to the right were three compost piles in different stages of decomposition. Tiny Baby was walking around between them, sniffing at this-and-that.

Paul grew below-ground crops in his front yard in order to keep his front yard food growing operation tactical. Having already grown some sweet potatoes in raised beds in his backyard, he couldn't wait to start planting them in the front yard. They had an attractive ivy-like appearance above-ground. Perfect for tactical food growing. Any passers-by would simply think they were just walking past a patch of ivy. Besides, with each summer getting hotter-and-hotter, it was getting easier to plant crops that were traditionally grown in the southeastern states. Paul even had some friends who lived near the small town of Gaston, Oregon, who were already growing their own peanut and tobacco crops.

However, he also realized that he needed to start rotating his crops in order to prevent disease, particularly with the Yukon Gold potatoes, which were going to be the staple crop in the event of a serious world-gone-to-hell event. Paul thought It was ironic that they cost more at the store than other common potatoes. They were ideally suited for the Pacific Northwest, hence their name. Each spring, Paul always saw the plants pop-up as volunteer ones, on his property.

The compost piles he continuously generated helped with this (and the weeds also) as he planted his seed potato each year in a thick layer of good, mature compost. Paul had convinced his wife years earlier that they were wasting seven dollars a month by having the city haul away their yard debris, particularly grass clippings from the lawn mower. Besides, the city was just going to make its own compost out of it, anyway.

I think I'll plant some more spinach here as well, Paul thought to himself. The generally dumb neighbors probably wouldn't even recognize the spinach plants, especially if the plants were scattered, instead of in rows. Paul loved fresh spinach. He also loved it cooked. At each harvest he would simply go out with a pair of scissors and cut the leaves at the base of the stem. Paul would either eat them fresh in spinach salads or simply chop-up the leaves and freeze them in freezer-grade Ziploc bags. Once the frozen spinach was thawed-out and cooked, you couldn't tell the difference between freshly picked, and frozen.

Also, the seeds were very easy to save. There were videos on YouTube demonstrating how to save seeds for any crop out there. In Paul's continual improvement as a survivalist, his priority of the last several years had been the study of seed saving in order to perpetuate his own organic, bio-intensive crops without any outside inputs. He and Emily had already confirmed that the amount of land their house sat on was a little over three-tenths of an acre and could easily produce a surplus of vegetables for them.

Besides, Paul sure as hell didn't need to learn any more about weapons and firearm technology. It seemed as if he had already possessed that knowledge as soon as he had popped out of the womb. Paul remembered a time when he was much younger, once explaining the functioning of someone's new rifle to them, that Paul himself had never even handled before. A lever-action Winchester. However in recent months he had been teaching himself gunsmithing on AR-platform rifles, since they were the single-most common American rifle out there. It was natural, coming from a paternal line of early-American Scotch-Irish who for the last couple of centuries had been non-stop farmers, cowboys, and soldiers.

Still kneeling at the garden with Tiny Baby eating some grass nearby, suddenly a series of quick bright flashes of light, brighter than the sun, came directly from the north. Paul started to turn to glance for a brief second -

"Oh shit."

Paul hit the position, going flat on his stomach, facing away from the flashes, face tucked to the ground, with his hands cupped over his groin. He lifted his head for a brief second to see new shadows being formed by the newer sources of light. He remembered this react-to-nuclear-detonation drill as an army infantry basic trainee from when he was 17, as if it had been taught yesterday. Except this time he didn't have to tuck an M16 under his body. There was no accompanying sound or blast wave, at least not during the time he was laying there.

"Oh my God." That's got to be the Puget Sound area, he thought to himself, referring to the vast military-industrial complex that stretched from Joint Base Lewis-McChord, just south of Tacoma, Washington, to Whidbey Island Naval Air Station, north of Seattle, and everything in-between. On the west side of Puget Sound, across from Seattle was the US Naval Shipyard in Bremerton. All this, in addition to the millions of people who lived in this densely-populated area.

He stayed there, still, for about a minute, waiting for any possible blast wave. It didn't seem like one was coming. Tiny Baby walked over towards Paul, then plopped-over on her side, looking at him. This was a cat's form of saying hi, with a big smile on their face. In a Pavlovian response, she must have thought the sun was coming out, with its accompanying warmth.

Paul grabbed the large cat, holding her to his chest. "Uh…no Tiny Baby. That was a nuclear detonation." Tiny Baby squirmed, just wanting to get loose, wondering why her human father was holding her like this.

Wow... This is it, Paul thought. The ultimate vindication, the ultimate reason for being a survivalist. The ultimate I-told-you-so. Time to turn-on what seemed like a lifetime's worth of mental, physical, and material preparation.

Shit, why didn't he grab her as soon as he saw the flashes? If these nukes had strayed off-course and been closer, she could have been turned into a projectile, even if *he* was still laying there. He got up with her, and ran towards the front door. He didn't have time to herd her back through the front door. Just as he got to the door,

Paul noticed a very warm breeze coming from the north.

Paul was almost giddy, like a little kid just finding out that he was going to Disneyland. Maybe Tiny Baby was being empathic. Cats were known for that, which was probably why they always seemed to want to hang around human couples, especially when those couples were being intimate.

Paul immediately got dressed in a pair of blue jeans, a brown T-Shirt and a coyote-brown, Marine Corps-surplus fleece pullover, followed by a coyote-colored pair of Danner GORE-TEX boots.

He went into his study, and opened a closet door. The door to a large gun safe appeared. *Beep beep...beep beep beep, ka-klunk.* Attached on the inside of the door was his Springfield Armory XD pistol in .45 ACP, already inside of its in-the-pants holster. He also grabbed a small stack of $100.00 bills from a shelf in the safe. He already had a change wad that he kept in his left front pocket, of ones, fives, and tens, along with 20's in his wallet.

Ridgefield, Washington was roughly 15 miles north of Portland, with Portland *hopefully* being only a secondary target, at best, since there was no significant military-industrial presence there. There were other reasons to target Portland, however: The city served as a concentrated transportation and shipping hub, between ship, rail and interstate highway.

He made a mental list of last-minute things he knew he needed to get at the nearby Walmart, based on having war-gamed this scenario on paper and in his head. There had been some good archived articles on last-minute shopping at Jim Rawles' *SurvivalBlog.com* website, which Paul had archived within his own digital files. Unfortunately, that particular stored information was about two broken netbooks ago. He had screwed-up by not making hard copies. Paul had no time to search for it now. Paul went into the garage, hitting the momentary switch for the garage door opener.

It didn't work.

Shit. EMP? He ran back into the house. Paul tried the light switches. Dead. The black, heavy MTM Military Ops watch on his left wrist was still working. His electronically operated safe obviously still worked. Thank God the safe also had a mechanical back-up. OK, the municipal power is gone. Paul ran back into the garage, and manually opened the two-car garage door.

Paul jumped into his nimble little white 1995 Nissan Pickup with its windowless fiberglass canopy. He had a certain sense of urgency but was not in a panic, where he would sacrifice safety. Paul backed-out of the garage, then got out of the truck to close the garage door and lock it with his house key. Thank God he had updated the old manual locking mechanism on the garage door with the current house key, months earlier.

As he drove, he knew he was going to experience idiots. Therefore he turned the anger on. This was part of the mental preparation that he wrote and lectured about with various preparedness groups.

When Paul parked in front of his local Walmart, it was like any other mid-morning shopping day. The parking lot had no unusual amount of cars parked in it. However, there were some people standing in the parking lot, and some in their cars, trying to get their smart phones to work. Paul didn't even know how to use one. He had spent his time learning how to grow food and improving the defendability of his house, the last several years. Although he had a separate degree in electronics technology and had once spent years as a skilled electronics technician, Paul didn't waste his time keeping up with consumer technology for two reasons: One, it was always rapidly being replaced by something else, and not always for the better. And, as a retired intelligence officer, he lived by the history-proven advice from Gene Hackman's character from the old movie *Enemy of the State*: Stay away from technology.

Paul got out of his small truck and walked quickly to the front of the large tan-colored store. He didn't want to convey a sense of urgency, just in case no one else realized what was going on.

Inside the store it was dark, except for light coming in through the skylights in the roof. It was a relatively light crowd of people, mostly elderly, overweight, some young tattooed couples, each with a small child-or-two, some of the men wearing a backwards baseball hat. Obviously unemployable, here to use their EBT card. Not that they had much to aspire to other than the usual availability of part-time, minimum-wage jobs.

Paul grabbed a cart and walked quickly to the pet food section at the back of the store. While he tried to slow himself down, he had always moved faster than the overweight, clueless, situationally-unaware crowd anyway, just due to his basic fitness level and sense of purpose, whenever he shopped. Get in, get what you need, get out. As he got a feel for the shoppers here, it seemed like they really didn't have a clue. Totally expected. Arriving in the pet food section, Paul grabbed five 20-pound bags of Meow Mix dry cat food, throwing two of them on the bottom rack near the wheels.

Luckily, Paul had recently conducted an experiment where he had pulled a 20-pound bag of Meow Mix from his larder. It had been vacuum-sealed inside a large Mylar bag, the date of storage written on it in black permanent ink, indicating just over four years of storage. He had opened it up and served it to their three cats: Mitten, a small black cat, Chubby, an elderly gray-and-white cat, and Tiny Baby. They ate it up, as if he had just brought it home from the store. Go figure. Meow Mix was like fortified junk food for cats: A corn product, embedded with flavoring and nutrients.

In a worst-case scenario, Paul had hoped that the cats would be able to supplement their own diet with local birds, mice, bugs, etc. However, he had seen Mitten (around the age of 50 in cat years) try to stalk game, and it was obvious that he couldn't catch so much as a cold. Tiny Baby, on the other hand, was a natural hunter and fighter, who already had her own confirmed kill of a bird, at six months of age. That would be the equivalent of a two-and-a-half year-old human being going out and catching their own dinner. She was truly a survivalist's cat. And if they were not up to it he could provide the small game for them with his 10/22 rifle, using sub-sonic .22 Long Rifle ammunition. His favorite was the Mexican company Aguila's *Super Colibri* round. Powder-less, but with a hotter primer than their regular Colibri cartridge, the bullet moved at roughly 500 feet per second. When fired from a rifle, it merely sounded like a pellet gun. However, in this case with many more foot-pounds of energy.

Paul then headed for the cooking oil section, buying as much olive and coconut oil as he could. He put several large containers of each into the cart. The coconut oil in particular would store almost indefinitely, and had numerous health benefits, even over olive oil.

Wait: Bread won't last long. OK, we need some, anyway. Besides, in their northern, Washington state climate, they could leave stuff outside in plastic milk crates, provided that animals didn't get to it, in the event of an indefinite power outage. Shit. What about nuclear fallout, Paul thought to himself.

Next, Paul headed towards the pharmacy and health area, grabbing large amounts of dental floss, soft tooth brushes, and toothpaste, along with regular antiseptic mouthwash (i.e. Listerine). He then went to get multivitamins - the potent formulas intended for older people. Then whole cases of meal replacement shakes (i.e., SlimFast) were next, along with whole cases of protein bars. These would be perfect in the event of a need for portable rations while patrolling, traveling, or any high-stress situation where highly nutritive yet easily digestible food would become ideal.

With his cart full, Paul headed towards the checkout. Move quickly. Don't worry if people notice, he thought to himself. Once there, there was a line of roughly ten people in front of him, with an elderly man and a young couple with a small child, the father looking like some gang-member wannabe, immediately in front of him. Nothing was going on. He left his cart, and walked up to the checkout.

"What's the hold-up," Paul asked.

"The card readers are down. We can only handle cash, right now."

"Is there an open register I can use? I've got cash. I can make exact change."

"Oh, OK, if you've got cash, then I can take you on the register over here." The checkout lady motioned Paul towards a vacant register behind her.

"Ma'am, do you mind if I help this gentleman over here," the checkout lady asked an older heavy-set woman in front of her.

"Huh? Oh yeah, that's fine."

Paul arrived with his cart, pulling the smaller stuff out of the cart while the checkout lady used a hand calculator to add everything up, organized into two groups: Food items, then state taxable items. He then paid for the groceries, and quickly exited the store.

As Paul headed out to the truck, he wondered if the stuff in the truck would be safe, while he went in for a second trip. It *should* be OK, since Paul had both tailgate and canopy hatch locks on the back of his small window-less canopied truck. After loading it up he went back for a second trip, this time thinking long-term storage and anything else he could think of, based on its storability.

When Paul re-entered the store, people were still clueless as to what happened, other than some minor panic over no cell phone service, or electricity. He headed straight for the emergency food section for #10 cans of various Augason Farms freeze-dried food items, along with square plastic buckets of rice, wheat, sugar and other staples. Then he grabbed mostly comfort foods. Foods like brownie mix, dehydrated strawberries, *more* freeze-dried beef, taco-flavored textured vegetable protein (TVP), etc. He also bought all the #10 cans of powdered low-fat and non-fat milk mix he could grab. Fortunately, Paul had recipes at home on how to make non-fat powdered milk taste more like real milk.

This time at the checkout things were visibly different. People were in a panic. Some were going back into the main part of the store to grab more stuff, while some left the store entirely. Paul had to brush his way past some of them as he headed towards the checkout. This time the checkout people were not even there, while even more people were standing in line. On another aisle, the store manager used his manual back-up key to open the register.

"Cash only, over here, The manager yelled-out to the crowd."

Several people went over to that checkout, most with their normal grocery shopping. Paul followed them. After a half hour, when it was Paul's turn to unload his cart, he was addressed by the person behind him.

"Wow, that's a lot of stuff there. Did you hear what happened," he asked. It was some white wannabe ghetto kid with a backwards hat on his head.

Paul, momentarily glancing at the kid, pretended to be oblivious. "Huh? No."

"You must have known about this, man. You look like you're in the military, or something."

Paul looked at him again. "Huh? Me? No. *I'm nobody.*" This stupid little fuck better not push it, Paul thought. He paid the several hundred dollars for the total, then continued loading his cart.

Upon seeing the hundred-dollar bills that Paul flipped through to pay the bill, the kid asked: "Hey, man, I was wondering if you could-"

"Hmm... No," Paul said, verbally cutting him off, looking off to the side, then straight at him while watching the clown's hands for any quick movement. "Get the fuck away from me," Paul told him quietly. The kid was already physically way too close to Paul.

The kid, sensing he was somehow in way over his head, just put his hands in the air. "Whoa, it's cool," and turned away.

Some of the other people looked at the kid, while some were still trying to get their smart phones to connect. Paul kept his eyes on him, in case he felt like drawing a weapon, or doing something else, as he finished loading his cart.

As he exited the store, pushing his cart, he thought, damn. OK, this will be the last cart. In front of him, he saw more people entering the Walmart. As he entered into the parking lot, he saw more cars arriving, with more people heading towards the entrances. He got to his truck, and started unloading the second cart-load into its canopied bed.

* * *

That same morning, Emily was writing computer code in her cubicle, when suddenly the connection to the remote server she was using went dead. After several minutes of wondering what was going on, the power in the entire building went dead...

"What's going on," several people said in unison. People began looking around at each other over the tops of their white cubicle walls. Great, Emily thought. I wonder how long this is going to last. I'll give it a couple of hours.

Emily was also in her early 50's, a couple of years older than Paul. She was slim and only slightly shorter than Paul, with cute, short brown hair and big brown eyes. Paul had made a good investment, he liked to brag to her when they were together, as she looked like a 50-something going on 30-something. Where Paul put more emphasis on athletic ability, Emily put more emphasis on diet and weight. Each was a perfect complement to the other's healthy living.

What should I do? Should I just leave for the day, Emily thought to herself.

Several minutes later a young, 30-something, dark-haired male security guard, dressed in black ran onto her office floor from the building's stairwell.

"There's an attack on the U.S. going on right now! It might be nuclear," he announced to everyone.

Emily wondered what her husband Paul was doing right now. Maybe she should find out what was going on herself. She immediately grabbed-up her personal belongings, taking the stairwell down to the first-floor, then walking out to the parking structure, where her bronze Toyota Camry was parked. She tried her smart phone from inside her car. There was no service available. That's weird, she thought. She remembered Paul saying something about a plan to rescue her in the event that something like this happened, if she actually needed him to retrieve her from Portland. However, the car started just fine and she did have the means to get home, so that was what she was going to do.

As soon as she turned out of the parking lot, traffic was tight. Gosh, I'm not even anywhere near the freeway, she thought. She knew a shortcut, however. She could head north on 99-W, on the east side of the Willamette River.

As Emily drove north, people were starting to appear from a nearby rescue mission. As she stopped at a stop light, a homeless guy with a brown-bagged bottle in his hand, waved at her.

"Yo mama, what be happenin'," he yelled, as Emily slowly passed in a long line of traffic. Fortunately, she could not hear anything outside of her Toyota.

* * *

Paul pulled into his driveway, now thinking about Emily in Portland. He got out to manually open the garage door, drove in, then got out and closed the garage door. Damn, he thought. He should have bought more comfort items, like cans of his Cherry Pepsi, for instance. He had learned a few years ago that he could store an entire 12-pack case of soda cans into a "Fat-50" ammo can. Oh well. He already had some of that in his crawlspace.

Paul noticed for a second time that all of his battery-operated electronics were still working: His watch, the electronic keypad on his safe. If the first wave of the strike were electromagnetic pulse weapons detonated in the atmosphere, wouldn't everything electronic have been taken out? Popular books on the subject suggested this, years before this attack. However, Paul also remembered the Quebec power outage of 1989, due to a coronal mass ejection. Although their power grid had been damaged, it didn't affect vehicles or individual devices.

Paul started putting the groceries away, not as normal, but on the floor in the spare room off of the garage that was dedicated to preparedness supplies.

What else should he do?

Emily.

Should he try to retrieve her from Portland? Paul had written a procedure for himself to follow, along with a list of what to load into a large ALICE pack with which to rescue his wife on his motorcycle. Great. He hadn't even pulled it out of the garage yet for the riding season. It needed an oil change and the battery and tires checked, just for starters. He went into the garage and remembered that he hadn't finished unloading the groceries from the truck. He could just leave everything else in the truck for now, using the Nissan pickup as a mobile storage container. He needed to call Emily. Good luck, he thought.

Paul went to his netbook and tried Skype. It showed no connection to anything. Wait: What if he went to a neighbor and used their land line? What neighbors? I don't know any of these idiots. He laughed to himself. He and Emily had lived there for almost 20 years and not gotten to know any of them. Emily was not the mingling type, and Paul, as a survivalist, wanted to maintain OPSEC (Operational Security). Her smart phone probably wouldn't be working though either, due to knocked out nodes from that possible EMP hit over North America.

Shit, I have to think of something, he thought. He walked quickly across the street to Frank and Wilma's house. He had always regarded Frank as a nerd. The low-key character in a movie. The technical character that was always used in a story to make the main character look cool. He was a short, somewhat pudgy guy, sometimes dressed in black trousers with a red shirt, with one of those phone devices sticking out of his ear. Paul noticed that Frank's little gray econo-box car was parked in front of his house. He happened to be home, as he usually was for lunch from his IT hardware maintenance job. When Paul knocked, he heard their large white dog barking loudly. Frank opened the door a crack, just enough to show his face, with the dog still barking loudly.

"Oh, hi Paul."

"Hi Frank. I was wondering... Do you happen to have a land-line phone, by any chance?"

"Yeah, we do, but we haven't been able to reach anyone. Do you know anything about what's going on?"

"No, not really. Would you mind if I tried my wife? I need to get a hold of her."

"Well, we've tried to make calls on it, and it's not working... I'm sorry that I can't help."

"OK. Well, thanks anyway," Paul said, trying to stay polite and pleasant. With that, Paul headed back to his house. What a little asshole, he thought. Paul had once invited him into his study, in order to show him the view from one of his windows, when some druggies at one time had been using the adjacent creekbed as an avenue of approach. Frank must already be in combat mode himself, wondering what Paul knew, and he wasn't about to let anyone into his house, period. Anyone. He had three daughters of whom he was very protective of, after all.

From Paul's research on his neighbors, he knew the guy was a devout Mormon. With an NRA sticker on the rear cab window of one of his small pickup trucks, Paul knew that Frank was himself a prepper. Paul actually liked Mormons in particular because they usually practiced what they preached, regarding preparedness. Paul had already tipped his own hand to the guy accidentally, between being seen running all the time or receiving UPS packages that appeared pretty heavy. Paul really didn't know what Frank thought of him. Paul figured it was probably somewhere between thankful for a fellow prepper living across the street, and worried. Although he and Frank had no issues, Frank probably didn't want to take a chance on someone coming into his house to jack them, or worse. Even with Paul, since Frank was probably a little intimidated by him, anyway.

On one occasion, Paul had noticed several vehicles with men visiting his house. He figured that if and when the proverbial shit hit the fan, Frank probably already had things coordinated with his church, or whatever it was the Mormons actually called them. Paul knew that some religious groups such as the Mormons were dead serious and stocked some pretty serious firepower of their own, as well as the other preps that they were well known for.

Frank was someone who Paul probably should have become friends with and shared preparation efforts. Paul hardly even considered it however, since their personalities were so different. Frank was the kind of guy who would step out of his house with a camera to use on a suspicious vehicle's license plate, while Paul would go out there with a five-pound sledge hammer, confront the driver and take out the driver's side window of said vehicle as a calling card, reminding the person whose neighborhood it was.

Frank probably grew up in his own home, with real parents, while Paul got to live as a second-class citizen in a miserable foster home where he got a head-start view of how the world really worked. Frank also seemed really wet behind the ears on a lot of things that Paul took for granted, such as knowledge of current geopolitical events and physical fitness. Not everyone gets to live across the street from a retired U.S. Army intelligence officer, Paul thought.

Paul and Emily once joked, laughing together about the possibility of Frank's preps.

"He's probably more prepared than you are," she once said, mockingly.

"Yeah, pudgy little Frank. When the shit hits the fan, he'll probably pull-out a semi-automatic Barrett .50 ready to go."

Paul stopped to think for a minute: Should he drive south into the East Bank area of Portland to check on Emily? He had told her on previous occasions that he would retrieve her on his motorcycle in the event of a societal emergency, *if* she needed him to. What if Portland is going to be hit as a secondary target? There was virtually nothing military in or around Portland except for an Air National Guard base and a couple of Army National Guard armories. Regardless, Portland served as a vital transportation hub along the West Coast. He knew that a ground detonation where the north end of the I-405 bridge and I-5 meet near Swan Island, above the rail yard and shipping docks below, would literally cut the West Coast in two.

This wasn't an option. If he couldn't reach her, of course he would go into SHTF mode, and look for her.

Survivalism wasn't just about keeping one's own ass safe. It was about caring for loved ones, regardless of whether or not it brought risk to oneself. The best thing that could happen is that he would arrive at her workplace just to find that she had left for the day, then find her at home, having suffered through no more than some worse-than-usual bad traffic. Paul wasn't worried about himself. He could get in and out of pretty much any situation, just as he had done in both Libya and Syria as a freelance military journalist. If he had to, he would take a raft back across the Columbia River and walk home.

Paul went back into the garage, now only dimly lit through a pair of translucent windows on the north-side wall of their house. He wanted to keep the large two-car garage door shut, until he was ready to leave. He took a look at his customized Kawasaki KLR650 motorcycle. It was parked in front of his small Nissan pickup at the back of the garage, stored for winter. He felt lucky having this 2007 model, as it was the last year for the traditional style of this originally military, dual-purpose motorcycle. The newer models of this bike, starting in 2008 were redesigned with flashy colors and nearly 50 pounds of needless add-ons, such as dual front disc brakes.

When Paul first bought this large street-legal dirt bike, it was black and covered with bright yellow and metallic decals. Now, his KLR650 was flat-sand colored, with OD green brush guards for his hands and a black tube-steel engine guard with built-in foot-pegs for highway riding. It was a godsend for long trips. All extra reflectors were removed. The chrome wheels had been subdued with Rustoleum-brand textured black spray paint. The Rustoleum paints worked surprisingly well on automotive applications. Paul had applied this paint directly to the chrome wheels after cleaning and roughing up the surface as best he could. He was surprised how well this paint stuck to bare chrome. The large, bendable, black turn signals were replaced with micro-sized turn signals, also painted to match the rest of the motorcycle. This helped reduce the overall physical signature of the motorcycle. Paul used an OD green, Condor-brand MOLLE fanny pack as a handlebar bag.

Although the motorcycle had a single-cylinder engine, with the addition of a little octane boost the large dual-use bike could take off like a rocket. On a short stretch of freeway, Paul had once gotten the bike up to over 100 miles per hour on a commute trip home from Fort Lewis, Washington.

Paul pulled the seat off the bike, and took a look at the battery. The electrolyte looked a little low after sitting throughout the winter months. After pulling the battery and filling each cell with battery acid solution, he reconnected the battery to its terminals. After turning the fuel valve to ON, opening the choke lever all the way and a few cranks of the starter, it rumbled to life. Thank God I didn't have to take the time to jump it, Paul thought. He had developed a method years ago of jumping a motorcycle battery using a car battery with the positive side of the jumper cable clamped around a screwdriver, which he then used as an insulated probe to contact the positive terminal on the motorcycle battery. Fortunately, he didn't have to waste that time, now.

While the bike was warming up for the first time in months, he checked the tires. Both were low, particularly the front tire. With a small one gallon electric air compressor, he topped them off. He also removed the license plate, which was wing nutted on the back of the bike. With the seat off, he removed the fuse for the headlight. Since he'd be in traffic, he left the brake light connected, for now.

OK, time to plan this, he thought. He shut off the motorcycle. Great, Paul thought. He had made a packing and procedure list, for the purpose of rescuing Emily from Portland. However, that was about two broken netbooks ago, which means that he had either archived it onto a DVD, or that it was still on the hard drive of a half-working netbook. Why didn't he make a hard copy of that? Years ago, he had put together a binder specifically for organizing hard copies of internet posts from Jim Rawles' SurvivalBlog website but had made hardly any hard copies of his own procedures, plans, packing lists, etc.

The good news: Paul had purchased a ruggedized 15 GB thumb drive from SurvivalBlog.com a few years earlier, pre-loaded with archives from that website. Paul had added his own stuff from other sources, as well. It was an amazing little thumb drive, completely metal-encased with a cylindrical screw-on cap that made the USB thumb drive not only waterproof, but electrically shielded.

He went to his safe, pulling out the .45 XD, attached to the inside of the safe door. There was already a loaded 13-round magazine in it, with the chamber clear. For safety reasons, Paul never carried a pistol with a loaded chamber. The philosophy he shared with other people was that he would rather be shot by a bad guy, than live with an accidental discharge, particularly if a loved one got hit.

Paul had trained himself in the Israeli method of simultaneously drawing and chambering a round. He also pulled out an AN/PVS-14 Night vision unit, complete with head harness. This had cost him $2500.00, but Paul was well aware of the force-multiplying effect of modern night vision devices. It was the best price he could get on those, as the price had originally dropped, then dropped some more. Paul had hoped that the price would have kept going down on '14's, as they were being made more available to the general public.

Paul then went out the sliding glass door in the dining room, into the backyard, toward the shed on the south side of the house. After unlocking the keyed-alike padlock on the shed door, he grabbed a black SUV tote off of a wooden shelf. He pulled out a US Army-issue MOLLE vest. This was the modern tactical vest worn over body armor by the US Army. However, this was not in the ill-conceived Army ACU pattern, or the incredibly popular MULTICAM that the US Army had transitioned to, for that matter. The same military contractor had produced a batch of these in an OD green-based woodland pattern for the earlier Battle Dress Uniform. Paul had been incredibly excited to come across these, as the OD green/BDU color pattern was much more suited to the temperate rain forest environment of the Pacific Northwest. The only thing he did not like was the black in the woodland BDU pattern, as anything black tends to stick out as an unnatural color in the visible world. Paul also knew that black stuck out like a sore thumb through night vision devices, both light amplification and thermal.

Paul also grabbed Emily's Condor-brand plate carrier, in OD green. His matching plate carrier was back in his study, next to the safe. Her matching motorcycle helmet in matte black was also on his "rescue Emily from Portland" list. He also grabbed one of his spare large-sized OD green ALICE packs, with improved SPEC-OPS shoulder straps, in sand color. All of Emily's stuff would go in there, along with extra ammunition, water and protein bars. Paul also grabbed a couple of sealed MRE meals, just in case they were further delayed getting back to Ridgefield.

Pro masks! If there is a hit on or near Portland, they could be a lifesaver, filtering-out radioactive dust, etc. Too bad he didn't have protective hoods for them. Wait! Emily's was in her car, in her get-home bag. His was in their storage room, in their preparedness area, with the dry vacuum-sealed goods. They were Finnish military-surplus M61 masks, with the left-side mounted, 60mm threaded air filters. He grabbed the dark OD green carrier, throwing a spare filter in with the mask and filter already in it.

It was crazy, Paul thought, possibly driving face-first into a nuclear detonation. *If* Portland was selected as a secondary target, that is. He went to the kitchen sink and filled a one-quart, then a two-quart jungle canteen. Damn! Water purification tablets. He'd need those too, if getting back to Ridgefield became difficult. In addition, there was a Nuke Alert key ring radiation meter and alarm, in another backpack. He put both into one of the outer pouches of the ALICE pack.

He just about had the ALICE pack together, to include his spare Army ACU Gore-Tex jacket for Emily. Wait: In the urban environment that Paul would be riding in, *he* should be wearing that jacket. If the Army digital ACU pattern was good for anything, it worked somewhat in downtown, urban environments. He put his older, hooded Army BDU pattern Gore-Tex jacket in the backpack for Emily. In the outer pouches of the ALICE pack were spare ammunition, three more .45 XD magazines, and the one-quart canteen. The two-quart canteen was in its carrier, attached with plastic coyote-colored MALICE clips to the side of the ALICE pack.

Wait: Ponchos? Poncho liners? These Army-surplus items were designed to be combined into lightweight, improvised sleeping bags. They would come in handy, in the event that they were delayed while heading back into Washington State. Or God forbid, something happened to the motorcycle.

Finally, one last thing: A handgun for Emily? He detached the frame of his Glock 17 9mm from a carbine conversion it was attached to, and put the slide back onto it. The Glock's frame had been DuraCoated flat OD green to match the Mech Tech Systems carbine conversion it had gone into, turning the pistol into a short rifle. The slide of the pistol was a creative, sprayed-on DuraCoat splash of OD green and coyote.

Paul grabbed two standard-sized, and two extended 31-round magazines, also in flat OD green. He grabbed two 50- round boxes of 9mm, putting them in the outer pouches of the pack, as well. Even if he didn't find Emily, the Glock would make a good back-up.

OK, now time to get dressed. Wait: I need a shower. Paul never put a motorcycle helmet on without first taking a shower. Fortunately, there was still hot water. Paul was already missing hot showers, as he took this one, knowing that this might be considered a luxury, in the near future. Just being able to stay clean was going to be important in the days to come.

After the shower, Paul put on one of his older brown Army T-shirts, and a set of Propper brand lightweight BDU's in solid OD green. He referred to this outfit as his "modern jungle fatigues." In the early 1990's, Paul had gone through the US Army's Jungle Warfare School in Panama, where his unit of the 101st Airborne Division (Air Assault) had gone for training, issued with the original Vietnam-era Jungle Fatigues. Many in his unit liked them so much, that they didn't bother to turn them all in, and were simply charged for them out of their next paycheck. Paul liked to dress up in this ensemble when selling his books at preparedness expos, etc.

Next went his good old black combat boots, leather dyed and brush-shined, with his trousers bloused inside of them. Although he loved his 100% Gore-Tex Danners, he didn't want to wear them out prematurely on the motorcycle. Then went his OD green plate carrier, with the MOLLE tactical vest secured over the top of that. Paul put his .45 in an angled, square-shaped MOLLE holster, attached on the lower right portion of the vest. On the left side were AR15 rifle magazine pouches. He decided to put his .45 XD magazines in there, for now. Paul was now a perfect blend of OD green and a little bit of old woodland BDU camo in the MOLLE vest. He looked like a cross between a Vietnam-era soldier and modern law enforcement. If this ensemble made him look too military, oh well. Better to appear as someone of authority if he does get noticed at all. Over all of this Paul tried putting-on his digital gray-green ACU Gore-Tex jacket. It didn't work. Great. He would have to wear the plate carrier and vest over it. Hopefully, no one of any real authority would notice him, if they weren't already overwhelmed with the current situation.

Paul felt that everything was as complete as it could be for this mission. If he forgot anything he would just have to improvise. He put his matte-black helmet on and being tactical, restarted the KLR650 in the closed, dimly-lit garage. It started up just fine. No dead battery here that couldn't hold its charge. He manually opened the garage door, pushed the already running motorcycle out onto the driveway, then closed the garage door behind him, locking it.

Another thing Paul loved about the KLR650 was the standard cargo rack, behind the passenger portion of the seat. For some strange reason, after all these years, the outer dimensions of the cargo rack *still* matched the inner dimensions of a U.S. Military ALICE pack's metal frame. All one had to do was simply slide the ALICE pack onto the frame and secure it, just like any other military scout had done with this bike, over the years. For this Paul used a large black bungee cord to secure the ALICE pack to said cargo rack: An extra one from his rain barrels, used to secure nylon window screen around the open tops.

It was now just him, his motorcycle, his ALICE pack, the handlebar bag, and what he was wearing.

* * *

The traffic in Ridgefield, Washington was no different than usual. Paul was worried as he rode the bike, as he had no means of drawing the XD while operating the motorcycle. He needed to be able to draw with his left hand, in order to actuate the front brake and throttle with his right. With the XD pistol mounted on the left side of his tactical vest, in addition to the fact that he didn't normally carry a round chambered, it was a complete impossibility, for now. If there was a reason to stop later, he could go through and re-adjust all of his gear. This should simply be the shock phase of this event anyway. He thanked God he wasn't living in some second-world country like Chile for example, where as soon as an earthquake started, the organized looting started.

Riding south into Portland was another story. As soon as Paul crossed the Columbia River Bridge on I-5, the freeways were now at a standstill in both directions. Paul was able to continue in the breakdown lane on I-5 South to I-84, going east. The Banfield, as this freeway was called, had now turned into a linear parking lot. No problem. Paul continued down the breakdown lane, in second gear. This lane was not blocked with traffic, *yet*.

Suddenly a beige sedan pulled to the right, into the breakdown lane, in front of Paul. There was not enough width here at this spot for a single vehicle to even travel in. The driver did it just to be an asshole, to try to negate the advantage of the motorcycle that the driver saw approaching in his rear-view mirror.

Shit! Standing on the foot-pegs, Paul skidded the large motorcycle to a stop, turning into the skid, like something out of a movie. The driver of the car just kept looking forward, as if he was oblivious. Dirtbag. Paul unzipped his ACU jacket in order to grab his .45 pistol and put half of its 13-round magazine into the driver through his rear window and driver's seat. Maybe the stupid fuck will notice this. Wait: Almost everybody in Portland packs something under the driver's seat, from fat little women with their .380 Auto's on-up. On top of that, Paul's side of the expressway was sided with a cement wall about ten feet tall. Even though he knew from experience at shooting ranges that the average Portlander couldn't hit the side of a barn with a firearm, half a dozen people could open up on him, with their rounds ricocheting everywhere and possibly hitting him. Paul decided against drawing a weapon.

Paul honked at the driver. There was still a gap between the driver and the cement wall that narrowed at the front of the car. Paul rode into the gap between the cement wall and the vehicle.

The driver of the car heard a hard tapping on his passenger-side window. When the driver turned his head to the right, he saw the barrel of a large caliber handgun pointed directly at him and a black motorcycle helmet with dark visor motioning him to move his car. Paul was able to do this at least, with the car itself blocking everyone's view. With that, the driver pulled back, into his lane.

"Yeah, you're one lucky motherfucker," Paul said quietly to himself, as he holstered the .45 and continued on.

I've got to get off this freeway, Paul thought. The exit for 33rd Avenue was coming up, less than a half-mile away. As he slowly continued in the narrow breakdown lane, he heard other gunshots being fired, in the distance. It seemed like other people were getting a head start on this new, collapsed world.

* * *

Paul finally arrived at Emily's business complex after using every sidewalk and breakdown lane. He parked the large motorcycle near the front of the main entrance to the glass-and-red brick building, making sure to turn and lock the handlebars. He un-fastened the ALICE pack off of the bike's cargo rack and put it on his shoulders.

Surprisingly, the main door was unlocked. Paul went inside and approached the security desk. Normally there was a black-uniformed security person at the chest-high counter-top. There was no one there. He continued into the building, going down a large carpeted hallway, then up a stairwell to an area where he was pretty sure his wife worked. When he got there, there was no one in their cubicles. He found the one labeled Emily Severn. It looked as though Emily had left, as well.

Paul then walked out to the cement parking structures that sat adjacent to the office building where Emily worked. He walked around on the first level of both structures, the large ALICE pack still on his shoulders, but didn't see Emily's car. She must have tried to get home. What path would she have taken? Should he try that path? Emily had once mentioned a route she would take, when the Banfield Expressway was backed-up. Paul had to at least try to find her on the way back.

Damn it, he thought. Paul needed to slow down. He needed to think. He needed to re-arrange his gear. He needed to be able to draw his XD pistol with his left hand. In the deserted parking structure Paul found an isolated corner, out of anyone's view. He headed back to the motorcycle, started it up and rode it there. Paul removed his TAC vest and re-positioned his holster on its MOLLE loops. Shit, he started thinking. Why didn't he just bring his VISM-brand shoulder bag instead of the vest? All that the vest was carrying was his pistol, and a few spare magazines.

In defiance of the modern military school of thought that placed emphasis on tactical vests, plate carriers, and going to one knee, if not standing, Paul placed more emphasis on how he had been trained years ago: Dropping flat on his stomach and fighting from the prone position. The one thing that the modern military typically had was 15-minutes access to the best trauma care in the world. The typical civilian survivalist, in a collapsed environment, would not.

Emily's bronze Toyota was *still* sitting on 99W northbound. Her car had not moved for at least 20 minutes, in this sea of vehicles that stretched as far as the eye could see, in all directions. The word biblical came to her mind. Paul had once warned her about this, something he called a linear parking lot, a phrase he had picked-up from that survivalist writer Jim Rawles. She remembered Paul once telling her that the population had been growing in the Portland area due to economic and climate refugees, particularly from California, as the state seemed to alternate between drought and flood. Gosh. Did he have to be so right about everything?

She realized that her Camry would run out of fuel even before she got out of Portland. She needed to turn around and head back to her office. There was at least one security person there, after all, and a cafeteria. Why did she even get on the road in the first place? Emily began signaling, in order to take a right around the city block next to her and return to her workplace.

* * *

The traffic on main surface streets, side streets, etc. was not moving. All of Portland was now a virtual parking lot. Riding on sidewalks and alongside cars, Paul looked for Emily's Toyota. Wait a second: Would she try to take I-5, or the Banfield Expressway to I-205? He had no way of knowing. Even if he did have his own smartphone, or whatever devices people were using nowadays, he wouldn't be able to communicate with her, in the first place. God, if only he had thought of giving Emily a GMRS/FRS walkie-talkie to keep in her car, set on an agreed channel, for emergency communications. He might have been able to make contact that way, once they got within range of each other.

Paul began heading east, then decided on Northeast 33rd Avenue, taking it north. As he passed cars, riding the sidewalk towards NE Killingsworth Avenue, he saw about six teenagers in the middle of the intersection.

"Yeah, it's the end of the world motherfuckers," one of them yelled, all of them wearing backward-facing ball caps. They were armed with a variety of hammers, butcher knives and screwdrivers, looking for stalled drivers to intimidate. The teenagers were looking into cars, kicking on the doors, banging on the windows, looking for some easy targets. Paul didn't see any other weapons. Cool, he thought. The first wave of chaos, perpetrated by gang wannabes. They didn't even count as small-time. Gee, I never saw this coming, Paul thought to himself.

Paul came to a stop at the corner of the sidewalk, at the southeast corner of the intersection, looking for an opportunity to cross the street. He kept his dark-visored, helmeted head turned towards the gang wannabes.

One of the teenagers looked at Paul from about 20 yards away, gesturing to one of his friends.
"Hey, what you looking at, muthahfuckah," he said to Paul. The entire group stared at Paul for a moment, wondering exactly

who or what he was, then slowly started heading towards him.

Paul simply drew his compact .45 XD with his left hand, then put it in his right. In a two-handed grip while sitting on the large motorcycle, he closed his left eye, lined-up the sights center-mass on the punk who spoke-up, then squeezed the trigger. BOOM! The punk fell backwards instantly. The rest of them simply scattered.

Paul then saw an opening in the cross-traffic in front of him, while holstering his pistol, as people reacted to his gunshot. He took it, going back up on the sidewalk on the other side of Killingsworth. He rode the motorcycle in front of McMennamin's Kennedy School, to his right. It was part of a chain of formerly disused and condemned properties, turned into restaurants and hotels. Paul loved the McMennamin's chain, a piece of Pacific Northwest culture that you just could not find anywhere else. Their on-site brewed beers were some of the freshest, most natural that anyone could drink. He loved drinking their Terminator Stout, smoking cigars in their cigar lounges, and eating there. Damn, those days are over now, Paul thought.

Paul continued up 33rd, all the way up to where it ended at Marine Drive, taking it west. He now had a chance to think about the punk he had just dropped. Getting shot, starting at this moment was an automatic death sentence. Damn, his first kill. He was starting to get nervous. It was justified, he thought to himself, in any legal sense, as there were more of them than him, and armed. Not that any of that would matter anymore.

Paul headed for I-5, knowing there was a bicycle path next to the northbound lanes starting at that interchange. He would try to keep an eye-out for Emily. Good luck, he thought to himself. He really needed to keep an eye on everything else, especially if someone wanted to jack him for the use of his much more mobile form of transportation.

Paul was thinking even more about Emily now. God, I hope she's safe, he thought to himself. As he got closer to I-5, Marine Drive was just another linear parking lot of cars and semi-trucks. Nothing was moving. People here were really panicking, filling the breakdown lanes with their vehicles. Paul had to use the dirt strips and sidewalks in front of the individual homes on that street, and again near a complex of Marriott hotels to his right. Paul then found the bicycle path as it entered a small tunnel He immediately took the bicycle path on it's way to Hayden Island, a large island on the Portland-side of the Columbia River. He saw the Hooters Restaurant and the rear of the Safeway supermarket on his right-hand side. What little he could see of the parking lot was packed with vehicles.

Paul then took the bicycle path interchange on Hayden Island to the I-5 Bridge, over the Columbia. There were people here, walking on the northbound pedestrian path of the old 1920's-built bridge. Paul had to lay on the motorcycle's horn to get people out of the way. As Paul headed towards one large group of people heading north, Paul hit the horn again. A heavyset older white guy wearing a white shirt and tie turned towards the approaching motorcycle, waving both hands above his head.
"Hey, hey..." the man yelled.

Paul simply down-shifted into neutral, slowing the bike down, and cross-drew the green-colored XD pistol with his left hand, pointing it at the guy trying to wave him down.
"Whoa shit. Jesus," the guy said, cringing, with both hands in front of his face. He and the rest of his group backed out of the way and made-way for Paul and the flat-sand painted motorcycle. Paul rode past, his pistol trained on them, his face hidden inside the full-face matte-black helmet with its dark-tinted visor. What was odd was that there was also heavy traffic heading south *into* Portland on the bridge, though not as much as was headed north, in the currently stalled, linear parking lot that the northbound side resembled.

Paul continued northbound in the walkway of the I-5 bridge, honking his horn to herd idiots out of his way. He then continued north on the grassy side of the breakdown lane on I-5 through Vancouver, Washington. Cars were now trying to use the breakdown lane themselves as an extra lane in a desperate attempt to get away from Portland.

God, he wished there was a way to get hold of Emily. Paul hoped she was at least able to turn the ignition off while stuck in traffic for long periods, so that she didn't run out of fuel.

There were no further incidents for Paul as he rode the large motorcycle in the grass on the side of the freeway, other than having to dodge honking automobiles, while heading home.

* * *

When Paul finally got home it was cold as usual, starting to get dark, and raining. Paul didn't like riding a motorcycle in the rain. He accepted that he did everything that he could under the circumstances, to try to find Emily. He had looked around in a sea of similar-looking cars trying to find her, only to discover that she had left her workplace. He was hoping that she would somehow make it home. He unloaded his rescue gear in his study, and went back out to finish unloading the groceries still in the truck into the preparedness room, off of the garage.

At this point, he was too exhausted to figure-out what next to prioritize. As an Army officer, he had been trained to prioritize. He used that same logical approach to everything, particularly survivalism. He had always wondered why the US Army didn't train all ranks in this type of thinking. During his prior service years as an NCO, he had had some excellent leadership training, but he was only exposed to this prioritizing decision-making model as an Army National Guard Officer Candidate.

His favorite visual model of this type of thinking was the original *Terminator* movie, where a list of Mission Priorities appear in front of the cyborg's internal visual display. In *Terminator II: Judgment Day*, John Conner wanted to go rescue his mom from a criminal mental institution. The cyborg simply replied, *Negative. Not a mission priority.* Paul had always thought that that was a cool scene. He also knew from the civilian corporate version in particular, that the ability to change the list of priorities as the situations themselves changed was also important.

He was still too tired to think of anything, but he knew that a lot of things needed to be done. He went into his study and started loading magazines for his M4 rifle, chambered in the Russian 5.45mm round.

Paul didn't just want a hyper-velocity 5.56mm round zipping through a bad guy without dropping him. 5.45mm Russian had a reputation for dropping people ever since the Soviet-Afghan War. The bullet of this round was a surprisingly complex design for something to have come out of a communist country in the early 1970's: Longer and skinnier than a 5.56 mm NATO bullet, with a steel-core behind a hollow cavity in its tip. Judging from its cross-view, it seemed as if the entire bullet was one big steel penetrator. It was specifically designed for even more yaw and tumbling effect upon hitting its target. Paul couldn't load as many of the Russian cartridges in each mag, due to the slightly larger .020 of-an-inch diameter of the tapered Soviet shell case. Most of his regular 30-round 5.56 mm magazines worked for the 5.45 mm, which was one of the reasons he loved this cartridge in an AR-platform. He also guessed that it was more accurate out of an AR, than an AK-74 rifle. It was no wonder that the Soviets kept their army's standard rifle round a state secret, until the Afghan war.

Another benefit of the Soviet-invented round was in the event that anything actually happened to Paul. Someone could easily assume his rifle took 5.56mm/.223 cal. If they tried to chamber one of those rounds into the rifle, it would instantly be rendered inoperable, unless they were good at extracting an entire stuck cartridge, in that case.

Paul also loaded magazines for his heavy, long-barreled AR15 and CAR-15 rifles with regular 55-grain 5.56 NATO. He loaded some magazines with all M855 steel penetrator 5.56mm and then a couple of others with 5.56mm Tracer. Using a piece of OD green duct tape on each magazine, he labeled these magazines with a magic marker, writing AP or TRACER on the tape. The tracer ammunition would make a good improvised incendiary round.

Next, Paul pulled out a .50 cal.-sized ammo can marked TRIPWIRE ALARMS in black Magic Marker ink. He took an inventory of his seven shotgun shell tripwire alarms. There was a surplus of tripwire spools, along with the necessary nails and pulleys.

What else? Should he start emplacing his coils of razor wire out there? He was too tired to think at this point and decided to go to bed. He couldn't stop thinking about Emily, however. He simply hoped she could make it back, either tonight or tomorrow. Paul was again dwelling on the idea that if he had just thought of having her keep an inexpensive FMRS/GRS walkie-talkie in her car, wrapped in some protective mylar with batteries removed but stored with it, on an agreed-on channel, this situation might have never occurred.

For the moment, they still had running water. Paul went to his bathroom, the small half-bath attached to the master bedroom, brushed his teeth with his electric toothbrush which still had its full-charge, as usual, and went to bed.

* * *

When Paul awoke he reached above and behind his head for his watch. The time was 7:42 AM on the hands of his large, heavy MTM Military Ops Black Silencer watch. He put the watch back on the headboard. Emily wasn't next to him in the bed. Just Tiny Baby, curled into a ball on top of the comforter.

"Emily" he yelled into the house, looking around.

No answer.

Shit.

Paul laid back-down in the bed. I'm going to have to go back into Portland, he thought to himself. Emily may have gone back to her office, due to the traffic. I hope she didn't get stuck, with the unthinkable happening, he thought to himself.

Paul got up, heading into the kitchen to make a cup of instant coffee. Great, I forgot: No power. All right. Paul went into his study and grabbed one of his cat stoves and a military-issue canteen cup, placing the one-ounce cat food can with holes in it on one of the electric grills on the stove-top in the kitchen, as he headed for the garage.

Paul came out of the garage with a small container of 91% alcohol. Paul poured a small amount of alcohol into the former cat food can, just to the bottom of the first row of perfectly drilled-out holes. After capping and securing the square plastic container of alcohol, Paul lit the small round stove with a match. Once it got warmed-up, he placed his canteen cup, half-filled with water, directly onto the cat food can-turned-stove. A nice, even blue flame surrounded the bottom of the canteen cup. He placed his hands over the canteen cup. The heat felt nice in the cold house.

Paul was reminded of the simple universal usefulness of a military-issue canteen cup. In Libya and Syria in particular, he had used it not only for boiling water like this, but also for reheating food and eating out of it. He also wondered how long the water would last in the pipes before having to use the adjacent creek. Paul knew he would soon be setting up his rain barrels, regardless.

With his coffee in hand, Paul started thinking about how he would work this next trip. This time I'm getting serious, he thought to himself. He went into his study and grabbed an OD green, MOLLE AR15/M4 rifle scabbard, made by the Chinese company NC Star. Normally considered bottom-of-the-barrel for tactical gear, they had made significant improvements in their soft products over the years. One of them was this particular nylon OD green scabbard. It had been specifically designed to accommodate every type of standard AR platform, from pistol AR's, to M4's, to full-length AR15's. Scabbards had once been issued to motorcycle troops, in the distant past. This was Paul's idea anyway, for his KLR 650. Paul had just never gotten around to figuring out exactly how he was going to attach the thing.

Paul then went to his safe, punched in the code, and opened it. He was trying to decide: His main battle rifle, the Russian cartridge-chambered M4, or his OD green DuraCoated CAR-15 in the usual 5.56mm NATO. If he got into any extenuating circumstances while in Oregon, he would need something in 5.56mm for compatibility.

All of Paul's AR rifles were completely DuraCoated in one solid coat of flat tactical OD green, to include the right side of the bolt carriers, and the inside of the dust covers. Even with the rifles in battery and engaging targets, they were still one solid unbroken field of flat OD green.

Tiny Baby came into his study and flopped onto her side, next to Paul's feet, while he was standing in front of his safe. He looked down at her.

"I got to go rescue your mom, Tiny. I can't play with you right now," he told her. She just rolled around, continuing to look at him. Paul squatted down to pet her and play with his feline daughter, anyway. She stretched her entire body, forming a straight line. It made him think of Emily even more, along with the fact that he liked cats more than he liked people, in general. He also realized that he needed to feed these guys.

Paul headed for the kitchen. After splitting a one-ounce can of food between all three of them and topping off their dry food and water, Paul squatted-down to pet them as all three were side-by-side, busily eating.

I should definitely save all these one-ounce cans now, Paul thought to himself. Then again, in this new world, he already knew that they would not be throwing anything away, period. Paul already had a mass-production system for turning these cans into alcohol-run cat stoves. He had downloaded one website's template for wrapping around each can, and drilling or punching the properly spaced holes. Paul regularly used a cat stove to heat water for his instant coffee, whenever he traveled to outdoor preparedness events or flea markets.

"Don't worry you guys. I'll protect you from the collapse of this civilization," he said to the cats as he got up from his crouch, while they continued eating. He was thankful that Emily had taken it upon herself a few months earlier to maintain a stockpile of several months of their canned food. This, in addition to the stored 20 pound bags of dry cat food should see them through a good couple of years of societal collapse.

Along with his coffee Paul had a bowl of cereal. Sitting at the kitchen counter on a tall stool, he used the time while eating to mentally plan this trip and its load-out. Then Paul got back to work. He grabbed his OD green and BDU-patterned tactical vest, filling it with the magazines he loaded the previous night. Almost all of the ammo was AP, along with one of his 30-round magazines labeled TRACER.

Suddenly he worried about security for the house while he was away. He couldn't keep people from trying to break in while he was searching for Emily. He did have an idea, though. He grabbed his ammo can containing the seven tripwire alarms.

Years ago at a certain website, on a page called Perimeter Alarm Systems & Accessories, Paul had purchased these .12 gauge tripwire alarms. They were basically a milled piece of aluminum holding a shotgun shell in place at one end, with a tripwire attached at the other. These devices had an internal firing pin mechanism that could be cocked back with a cotter pin connected to a tripwire. When the tripwire was pulled, it released the firing pin and fired a blank shotgun shell straight up into the air. A non-lethal CS, pepper spray or signal flare round could also be used legally in these devices, before the collapse. They were designed to be nailed into a solid wooden surface, such as a tree or any other structure. They could also be zip-tied to smaller objects, such as metal poles or small tree branches.

Paul decided to modify this arrangement. Before the collapse he had also bought some small wire pulleys, one for each tripwire alarm. The smallest pulleys that he could find at his local Home Depot store were designed for awning cables. These pulleys were not only solidly built, but were swiveled at their top mounting hole, making them perfect for relieving the stress on a bent tripwire. The tripwire could then be bent at virtually any angle in order to aim the device anywhere that Paul wanted, such as back in the direction of the tripwire. Then, he purchased not only more 12 gauge ammo, but 3-½" .00 magnum loads, dedicated to these devices. These were always in stock at various stores, since these shotgun cartridges were actually too long to chamber in most shotguns, with their three-inch chambers. Against any tree, fence-post, or by driving a couple of wooden stakes into the ground, he could emplace these devices anywhere he wanted.

Paul felt that these devices were far safer and convenient to operate than making them out of mousetraps. In the final step of arming each device, all one had to do was to carefully slide the .12 gauge cartridge into place through the milled slot at the front end of these devices, then walk away. Paul made a note to wear both hearing and eye protection while doing this. He also referred to these as his little "mini-Claymore mines."

Paul set three tripwires along the three outer sides of their awning-covered deck, assuming that anyone who came into the back yard would walk onto it. Using the pulleys, Paul stretched the military-surplus tripwires horizontally at ankle height, then straight-upward to about waist-height, where the devices were emplaced, with a slight upward aim. As a finishing touch, he used white spray paint on the devices, in order to camouflage them into the wooden vertical beams of the deck where they were nailed.

Paul didn't like the idea of aiming the devices directly at the house, but he didn't want to start putting nails into the side of the house, in order to aim the devices away from it, especially if they didn't get tripped, which ideally was what Paul hoped for.

The final touch was a sign made on a sheet of printer paper. With a red magic marker, he wrote:

DANGER !!!
TRIPWIRED TRAPS
ON DECK !!!
<u>DISARM !!!</u>

He taped the handmade sign on the inside of the sliding glass door, all four corners. This was not just to alert Emily in case she came home, but also to remind himself that they were there. With both six-foot wooden backyard gates padlocked from inside the backyard, the sliding glass door was usually the only point where Emily or Paul would enter the backyard deck. There was another exterior door to the back yard in the laundry/storage room, but was rarely ever used.. Even if any bad guys *did* notice the warning sign taped to the inside of the glass before setting-off any device, it was better than Paul or Emily accidentally tripping one of these devices, themselves.

It's time to get my game-on, Paul thought. He grabbed the AR rifle scabbard out of his study, and went out to the garage to test-fit the scabbard on the motorcycle, thinking maybe across the handlebars. It didn't work on the handlebars... Wait! Paul took the shoulder-strap that came attached to the scabbard and draped it around, and underneath the front of the frame and fuel tank. With the help of some OD green duct tape, he now had the scabbard sitting on the side of the KLR 650's fuel tank, similar to where a cowboy would have his rifle scabbard placed in front of him on the side of a horse. This was too good to be true, he thought. He went back into the house to retrieve his CAR-15 carbine and tested the arrangement by putting it inside the scabbard.

Yes! Paul was excited by this new discovery of his. The ultimate test would be to actually ride with it and draw it one-handed from the scabbard. If it didn't work he was bringing the roll of OD green military duct tape along, anyway.

Paul grabbed the ALICE pack off the frame of the bike and re-inspected the contents. He couldn't think of anything to add to it, except maybe a couple more MRE's.

The big difference this time would be firepower. He would also bring the Mech-Tech Systems carbine upper for Emily's Glock 17, which she always kept in her Toyota. Emily should be able to transition to the carbine conversion, since she was already accustomed to her Glock 17 pistol, he thought. It had a good, large heavy-duty electronic reflex sight on top of it. Paul made sure there was a two-point sling attached to it. There were already two fully loaded extended 9mm Glock 31-round magazines for it. Paul stuffed these into one of the ALICE pack's outer pouches.

Should he wait until tonight to move out? No. That would just be wasting time, Paul thought. Everything was in order. It was just a matter of going back into the zoo that Portland was in the early stages of becoming.

* * *

Traffic was a little better getting back into Portland. Paul didn't even have to use the sidewalks and breakdown lanes, *as much* as before.

As Paul arrived back at Emily's workplace, a man was wandering aimlessly along the sidewalk in front of the business complex, near the entrance to the parking lot, yelling at passing cars. He was obviously homeless before this, long hair with a beard, and a dirty old blue down jacket and jeans. As Paul rode past the man, he noticed that several cars were now parked in the portion of the parking structure nearest the building where Emily worked.

"DON'T YOU PEOPLE KNOW WHO I AM? I'M GOD!" The bum continued yelling at cars as Paul pulled into the ground-level of the cement parking structure.

Yes! Paul saw Emily's car there!

"I SAID I'M FUCKING GOD," the bum repeated, looking in Paul's direction.

Paul brought the motorcycle to a stop near the cars parked there as the crazy homeless person looked at him. The bum simply stood there, staring at Paul from about 40 meters away.

"YOU! WHO ARE YOU? I CAN'T SEE YOUR FACE," the bum yelled, pointing his finger at Paul. "YOU'RE THE DEVIL! I CAN'T SEE YOUR FACE! YOU'RE THE FUCKING DEVIL." He continued yelling at Paul, with a contorted, angry look on his face. Paul just simply sat on the KLR 650, shaking his head and laughing at the guy. Then, the homeless man began walking towards Paul, drawing a large kitchen knife from his jacket.
"YOU'RE THE DEVIL!"

Paul, still sitting on his bike with his helmet on and dark visor still drawn shut, calmly pulled the CAR-15 from its OD green scabbard. He popped the rear MBUS sight up, without bothering to extend the stock and leveled it at the bum's head, flipping the selector switch to FIRE.

"Oh shit," the bum said to himself, stopping in his tracks, lowering the knife.

BOOM!

The back of the bum's head literally exploded as he fell to the pavement, on his back.

"Damn."

* * *

"Oh my God, what was that," one of the employees in the building exclaimed.

Several people, including Emily went to the south-facing windows, to see what the sound was. They were nervous, as they had been hearing gunshots off in the distance, all day. As they looked down at the parking lot from their third floor, they saw a man lying face-up on the pavement, with a large pool of blood forming where his head lay, while someone not far from the man sat on a motorcycle, removing his matte-black full-face helmet, along with some earplugs that he had in his ears.

"That's my husband," Emily said aloud to no one in particular. She recognized the flat sand-colored motorcycle, and the black helmet. She pounded on the thick glass window, using the palm of her hand, hoping Paul would hear it. He didn't seem to. She ran for her cubicle, and started collecting her things, back into her get-home bag. Wait: I better go out there to meet him, she thought. Emily was so excited and so relieved, she couldn't think straight. She ran for the staircase in the building, going as carefully and quickly as she could, holding onto the staircase's handrail for dear life.

Paul locked the motorcycle helmet to its lockable hook next to the seat, re-positioning the CAR-15's double-point sling onto his right shoulder, with his right hand on the pistol grip, old school. Paul never understood the limp-wristed Iraq Occupation-style of holding a rifle. Paul thought it looked gay. How many times could you reinvent holding a 50 year-old rifle on your body? Not that he had anything against gay people.

As Paul approached the main doors to the building, Paul saw someone inside the glass wall, running for the door.

It was Emily!

Paul broke into a run as Emily opened the large commercial glass door for him.

"Hi Sweetie," she said excitedly.

"Hi Sweetie!"

"I'm so glad you made it," she said, as they hugged each other.

"Me too. We need to get home."

"OK. I just need to go get my stuff."

"OK. Hey, I just thought of something. Let me go grab the bike, so I can park it inside here."

"I don't know if you're allowed -"

"Uh, Sweetie... Yeah, it's OK," Paul said, nodding his head slightly. Emily was locked-on with Paul, understanding the need to prep, but was also all about following the rules, during *normal* times. She just needed to catch up a little here. Being married to him all these years, she knew Paul didn't necessarily follow the rules, anyway.

"OK. I'll hold the door open for you," she said.

Paul ran back out to the bike, unlocking the helmet so that the rear tire would not scrape against it, resting its chinstrap on the handlebar. He got on it, starting its engine, heading for the glass doors. Paul aimed the bike and was able to very slowly make it in, working the handlebars, the rear-view mirrors just barely clearing the door-frame. Emily pulled the door shut behind him.

"What happened out there," she asked.

"Some guy thought he was God and that I was The Devil. He was wrong on both counts," Paul said, getting off of the motorcycle, locking the motorcycle's handlebars, as an extra precaution.

"Oh my gosh..." she said quietly, putting her head in her hands. She was not used to seeing this sort of thing. At least not in the real world.

"Let's go get your stuff."

* * *

"I almost twisted my ankle on these steps, I was in such a hurry to let you know I was here," Emily told Paul, smiling.

"Well, we can take our time now, sweetie. I hate to sound like a nerd, but we need to keep things safe now. We can't afford to get injured," Paul told her as they walked up the staircase, giving her a kiss on the cheek.

"Isn't there some security guy that's supposed to be here?"

"He was the first of us to leave, then he returned like me and some of the other people here. He secured the building for us and let the other workers in. When the traffic started to improve a little bit he said he needed to get home. A lot of people came back here because of the traffic jam everywhere."

They walked into her cubicle area, where her co-workers all turned to look at them. A few were startled, as they saw Paul's ensemble of tactical vest, plate carrier, ACU Gore-Tex jacket, bloused OD green trousers, black boots and large military ALICE pack. Paul expected to see nothing but a bunch of nerdy, preppy techno-geeks. However, they were of all ages, from 20 to 60-somethings. They were dressed in mostly casual clothes.

"Hi, are you law enforcement," someone asked. He was a slightly chubby 30-something guy with nerdy-looking small square glasses. At least they would have been nerdy back in Paul's time, anyway.

"What's going on out there? Is the traffic thinning-out now?" another one of Emily's male co-workers, a guy who looked to be in his 50's, asked.

"Yeah, a little," Paul replied. As he watched Emily put the last of her office things into her own backpack, the crowd of office workers began noticing the solid flat OD green-colored CAR-15 slung on his right shoulder, muzzle down.

"We should have enough room for everything that you want to take back home, between your bag and mine. Remember, you're not coming back here."

"What about my car?"

"We'll try to come back for it later."

"What do you mean," a heavy-set woman about Paul and Emily's age asked, as Emily picked up her get-home backpack.

An older woman in her 60's came up to Paul and Emily.

"Oh, I don't know if you recall, but I think we met at the party we were all at, about a year ago. You're a writer, right? You wrote a book? About something like this happening?"

Paul turned to her. "Yes Ma'am, I did," Paul said to both women, with a pleasant expression. He didn't want to be a totally cold asshole, here. They all seemed like decent people.

A young Chinese guy approached Paul. "Do you know what's happening? We heard that there's an attack on the US going on."

"I'm not sure, but I think we've been hit with a nuclear strike," Paul said. The small crowd began murmuring among themselves. The 30-something-looking guy spoke up again.

"Are you law enforcement, or something?" The same guy with the nerdy glasses, repeating his question.

"I'm nobody. Just somebody who saw this coming," Paul replied. He turned back to Emily. The other office people were looking at Paul, and continuing to murmur between them.

"OK, I think that'll do it," Emily said.

"Are you sure you got everything?"

"Yeah," Emily replied. It wasn't much. Just her paperwork, and photos. It didn't even fill-up a three-ring binder. It only took her about 30 seconds.

"OK, let's go," Paul said. Emily began saying goodbye to the coworkers in her work group as Paul looked out the window toward the parking lot area. It took only seconds, as Emily had once explained to him that she didn't actually interact with them. Only with other people at remote locations, which is why she was able at times to work from home.

* * *

By the time Paul and Emily reached the main lobby of the building, they both had matching matte-black full-face motorcycle helmets on, this time with clear visors. Paul had packed these as well.

"I think I'm going to be sick," Emily said. At a distance, she saw blood from the back of the long-haired bum's head, heading for a sewer drain. "Did you have to shoot him?"

"He was 'gonna introduce me to his large kitchen knife, Sweetie. See? The big kitchen knife over there," Paul explained, while pointing to it in the distance.

"Oh my gosh..."

With their gear secured, Paul got on the bike, started it up and turned it in a small circle. He began inching it through the entrance of the building's main lobby, until it was once again outside.

"OK honey child, get on," Paul said, with a happy voice.

"How can I get on? You've got your backpack there on that rack, with mine on top of it."

"Just kick your leg over the seat and slide on. I'll lean forward a little bit. It'll be tight, but once you're on it'll act like a big backrest for you, just like being in a car."

"OK." While holding onto Paul with both hands, Emily managed to get her right leg resting on top of the seat and little by little was able to hop on her left foot, onto her half of the tall dirt bike-type seat. Paul tried to help a little bit, learning the motorcycle in her direction.

"OK, hold onto me."

Emily threw her arms around his waist. As they took-off, traffic had lightened up considerably, but it was still like the a late-afternoon rush hour. He was still going to have to use some creative methods to get the two of them home, regardless.

* * *

It was still gridlock, trying to head north out of Portland. It was now due mainly to accidents and stalled cars stemming from arguments, shootings, etc. Some of the stalled vehicles had bullet holes in them. They headed north on I-5, riding in the breakdown lane, worming their way around abandoned vehicles. Paul decided to pull off of the freeway near Delta Park, going through a barrier-less stretch and off-road over some open grassy area underneath Marine Drive. Paul aimed the two-person, cargo-laden motorcycle towards the small tunnel there, where he had been the previous day.

"What are you doing," Emily yelled at Paul, as he slowly rode them down a steep, yet short embankment straight down, carefully working both front and rear brakes. He turned a sharp left, entering the tunnel, then killing the engine. He turned his helmeted head towards Emily.

"The pedestrian walkway might have more people on it now, trying to get out of Portland. I need you to get off of the bike for a second,"

"I don't know if I can."

"Just search for the ground with one of your feet, then hop off of the seat."

Emily tried, her left foot finding the ground, turning her body toward the seat with her right foot still on top of the seat. As she hopped backward on her standing leg, she fell backwards onto the ground, her backpack breaking her fall as she landed in a sitting position.

"Oh no. Are you OK?"

"No,... I just fell."

"I'm sorry, Sweetie."

Paul was glad he was still wearing his full-face helmet, since he was trying to hide a small smile. He knew Emily was healthier than most women her age and could handle a small stumble.

"We need to get your Glock out of your backpack. Now that you know how to hang on, I need you with a weapon to help cover us while we cross the bridge." Paul then got off of the motorcycle himself.

"How am I going to hang on to you with my gun in my hand?" They both still had their helmets on, facing each other in the small pedestrian tunnel.

"Just do it like this." He demonstrated for her by holding the Glock 17 in his right hand, trigger finger extended along the slide of the pistol. With his left hand he pretended to be holding onto someone's clothing in front of him.

"And by the way here, load this," Paul said, as he handed her a loaded, extended 31-round magazine for her pistol.

"OK."

They each got back on the motorcycle and continued their trip along the paved bicycle path. Once they got to the I-5 Bridge, there were not as many groups of people walking as Paul had encountered the day before. Still, he was cautious, using the motorcycles' horn to warn people of their approach.

As Paul rode them tactically along the breakdown lane and grassy side of I-5 North through Vancouver, Washington, nothing serious occurred, other than their amazement at the number of vehicles bumper to bumper on the freeway. The word "biblical" came to Paul's mind. Their ride was bumpy and slow, yet fast relative to the little-to-no movement of the freeway traffic.

* * *

Back inside the house after putting away their backpacks, the first thing Paul did was point out the sign he left on the inside of the sliding glass door. Then he invited Emily out on the deck to show her his devices and the tripwires that were attached to them.

"Oh my gosh, I can barely see them," Emily said as Paul pointed along each wire and the white-washed, 3½ inch .12 gauge cartridges and firing devices.

"Why don't we go back inside. I'm gonna disarm these guys now." After they both went back in, Paul came back out on the deck, this time with a hammer, wearing headphones and clear protective eye-wear.

"I'll show you how to disarm these things." While Emily watched from the sliding glass door, Paul simply crouched behind each device and gently slid the .12 gauge cartridge out of each one. "That's all there is to it. To arm them, the very last thing you do is simply slide the round back into the slot. I'll be re-deploying these little guys around our perimeter. I'll only deploy these in spots where we know a bad guy is likely to enter or climb-over. I'll also rope the areas off with signs on our side of these devices."

"Well that's good," Emily said. Paul then used the claw-end of a hammer, prying the firing devices from where they were nailed.

Paul followed Emily into the living room, where they both plopped onto the couch together, each taking the opposite corner, facing each other, while taking a breather.

"Well, our first priority is water," Paul said. "I'll grab the Big Berky out of the attic, and set-up the rain barrels in the backyard. We've got several other ways to treat water besides the British Berkfeld. We've got those bottles of Polar Pure, and our individual water filter systems. We can even use bleach, if we have to."

"Oh wait," Paul continued. "We need to worry about radiation. If we retaliated against targets in Asia, we might not get direct fallout, but there could be some residual radiation drifting over us, similar to what happened after Fukushima, except maybe worse."

Emily was thinking about security. "How much of that razor wire do we have?"

"We have ten roles of it, along with an old surplus roll of used concertina wire, *and*, a 100-foot bobbin of good old barbed wire from Home Depot." Paul remembered Jim Rawles' instructional novel *Patriots: A Novel of Survival in the Coming Collapse*, where in the story, defensive wire became literally worth its weight in gold.

"What about the cats," Emily asked. "Mitten likes to climb the fence in the back yard. He could get seriously hurt."

"Wow. You're right, come to think of it."

"We also need to bring all the stuff up from underneath the house and store it in the storage room so we can get to it," Emily said.

"Yeah, all the beans, bullets and band aids' stuff." As Paul ended that sentence, another realization came to mind. "Oh shit,...literally."

"What?"

"Sanitation. That needs to be priority number two."

"What, you mean over security?"

"The toilets probably aren't going to be flushing much longer. We need to dig a latrine, starting now."

"Where are we going to do that?"

"In the north side of the back yard, as far away from the creek as possible. I think it's just about 100 feet from the creek. Right there at the northwest corner of the fence. Digging a six-foot hole is priority at the moment. We've already got a couple of sealed toilet seat ensembles that'll fit a five or six gallon bucket. I'll cut the bottom out of one of the buckets. We'll figure out how to construct the rest of it later, using pallets, tarps, whatever. Also, keep in mind that this is going to be a dry hole. We'll be pissing into a receptacle and returning all that sterile nutrient to the compost piles, rather than creating a bio-hazard stew underneath us. We can use one-gallon plastic milk jugs for that, with a larger hole cut in the top, just like the compost bucket, under the kitchen sink. Just think of it as part of our closed-loop, bio-intensive gardening system. Hopefully, we can keep the whole thing sealed up with something like the window screen material we have on hand and keep all the flies away from it."

"Uh... No, I don't think so. I'm not going out into the cold just to use a toilet," Emily replied dryly.

Paul then took a minute to think about this demand of Emily's. "OK, we use the bucket toilets indoors with some dirt in them, but I'll still dig the hole, and that's where all the dry waste will go."

Paul was somewhat familiar with humanure, or human waste composting. However, it was a very involved process, and even with the properly composted waste, it still could not be used to grow food crops. Some people added human waste to their bio-gas generators, in order to produce usable methane gas, but this again was an even more complex process, way beyond the scope of their current needs.

Paul was also aware of the use of permaculture, where sewage treatment was achieved through natural processes, using local vegetation and aquaculture, for small communities. However, this could normally only be done by experts in that field and was definitely something that Paul only saw happening on the other side of this collapse, anyway. This was assuming that people with those particular skills even made it to the other side of this bottleneck, or human die-off.

"If the situation permits later on, I'd still like to place a real porta-pottie over the top of the hole, with a hole cut out of the bottom of it and the urinal portion diverted into a container, like a one-gallon milk jug, or onto the newest compost pile. In the meantime, we'll go with your plan," Paul told Emily.

"OK, good."

"Cool. With all the other neighbors being clueless, there's already going to be a sanitation crisis, generating diseases like cholera, dysentery, etcetera. During that phase, we're going to need to limit our interactions with them, as well. We also have an Army field manual on sanitation that we might be able to get some good ideas from. I know this sounds bad, but based on what we know of our immediate neighbors they don't really have anything to offer us anyway, as far as working with them in any real way is concerned."

"Sounds like a lot of work."

"Yeah, it will be. Why don't we just get some rest today and we'll get started on this stuff tomorrow. I'll dig the latrine pit while you start grabbing stuff from under the house and start organizing it with the rest of the supplies in the storage room."

"OK."

"Wait," Paul said. "We need to worry about radioactive fallout, even if Portland doesn't get hit. It could arrive from overseas. Everything in the Seattle area north of us should drift directly eastward. That's what happened when Mt. Saint Helens blew, anyway. Either way, what's now happened is going to add to the background radiation all over the planet. I don't know when it'll arrive, but we need to be prepared to seal-up the house, at least. Do we have any indoor plants?"

"A couple."

"Well, that's better than nothing," Paul said. "We can exchange CO_2 and oxygen with them for a period of time, anyway. I'll have to go all around the house with plastic sheets and duct tape to seal-up all the openings in the roof and the attic."

* * *

When they woke up the next morning, after having had some intimate time together, Paul and Emily stayed in bed, facing each other, talking.

"I'm kind of worried about those spools of razor wire you put out on the deck. Where were you going to string them?" Emily asked.

"Just below the tops of the fence, on our side so that no one outside the house sees them, except for a bad guy: at the last second, or when he notices it too late. That's when we engage them with weapons fire. I don't want to make it too obvious, at this stage."

"Yeah, but won't that hurt the cats? Mitten likes to climb and walk along the fence."

"Wow, that's right," Paul said.

"Mitten always climbs the fence, to get back to the house in that one corner of the fence you're thinking of."

"You know, you're right," He knew that Mitten liked to explore at night. The small black cat even had a strange simian type of intelligence. Whenever he wanted something, he always looked at Paul or Emily with an intent look on his face. Instead of meowing, he actually enunciated sounds, such as a faint hiss or gasp, with his mouth open, as if he were actually trying to mimic human speech, exhaling over vocal cords that didn't exist. Paul had nicknamed him Cornelius, from Roddy McDowell's Dr. Cornelius from the original movie *The Planet of the Apes*. Paul's adult son, who lived in California and would visit once in a while, totally understood his father's logic: He really is a Cornelius, he once said.

Paul began thinking of his son, Christopher. He was from Paul's first marriage. He was 30 years old now and was living with his mother in the Sacramento area, working as an unarmed security guard. He was a pleasure to spend time with. Paul really missed him, since it had been roughly a year and-a-half since he last saw him. He had always told Chris that he needed to head back to the house in Washington State, in the event of any large-scale societal event. He hoped he could make it, somehow. Even with Paul's tactical and technological capabilities, a rescue mission all the way down to California would be extremely risky.

Emily interrupted his thoughts.

"It's just not worth the risk of the cats getting hurt by those long barbs. It even snagged me once, just standing out there on the deck, next to those unopened spools. We might not have access to a vet, she said."

Paul, laying on his side with his head leaning on his elbow, looked at Emily.

"I know where he uses the fence and where he doesn't. I can string the first rolls of the stuff on the other areas of the fence and along the ground, in the back yard, in triple strands or whatever. That way the cats can safely avoid the stuff. At least it'll canalize anyone into a more visible area or into one of my little goodies. Later on, I can be more aggressive with the stuff. Besides, cats have good instincts for avoiding sharp barbs, trip-wires, stuff like that, Paul continued. Even if they bumped into the wire, they probably wouldn't generate the foot-pounds necessary to trip the wires."

* * *

When they finally got up, they realized there was only a trickle of water coming from the bathroom faucets.

"Oh great," Emily said , from the main bathroom.

"We need some drinking water. We've got some under the house."

Paul then went back into their bedroom, opened the entrance to the house's crawlspace and went in. When he came back out, he had two clear, two-liter pop bottles full of emergency water. They had each been treated a couple of years earlier with four drops of chlorine bleach. He poured some into a glass and tried it. It tasted just fine!

"Want some coffee or tea?" Paul asked as he went into the kitchen, ready to boil a full canteen cup of water with his small alcohol stove.

"I'll probably have some tea."

Since Paul was boiling water for two people, he thought he'd go out to the backyard shed and retrieve his Kelly Kettle.

Paul had just purchased the Kelly Kettle, which basically used the water poured into it's outer design as the insulator of a small rocket stove. The smallest of the three sizes, this one would heat just more than enough water for two people. Paul suddenly had an idea. Since he was going to be boiling some water anyway, why didn't he just get it from the creek, next to the house?

Already inside the shed, He then grabbed a military surplus five-gallon plastic jerry can, and a ladder, leaning against the house. He'd use that to make hopping the city fence bordering their front yard a little easier.

After dropping the filled water container back in their front yard, muscling up and over the short cyclone fence, Paul then went to the woodpile and grabbed a bunch of small twigs and sticks out of a plastic milk crate. In recent years Paul had placed more priority on storing twigs and small fallen branches. He had been migrating more towards biomass-fueled, rocket stove-type devices, with their roughly 90-percent efficiency.

This was one of the reasons Paul had replaced his 16-inch two-stroke engine chainsaw with a 14-inch electric one. The newer electric one required no liquid fuel, which would also have to be mixed, and was much easier to operate. Just perfect for a suburban setting.

One of Paul's biggest priorities as a survivalist was in not creating a self-fulfilling prophecy: in other words, safety hazards. In previous years he had seen too many survivalists' retreat homes burn down, for instance, or their children killed while playing in a trench that was dug for an underground shelter. The electric chain saw represented that much less fuel that he had to store on their property, along with the fact that he could run it off of his alternative electricity system or any other high-wattage power inverter that was connected to a car battery, for instance.

Paul also grabbed a single hollow cinder block near their covered woodpile and brought it onto their backyard deck. He sat it on its side, setting the the Kelly Kettle on it. Paul made some tinder out of a small ball of old dryer lint and some discarded wood stain, dropping it into the hollow-shaped kettle, followed by some small sticks and twigs. After taking a match to the tiny lint ball a nice fire was now going through the center of the kettle, Paul warming his hands over it. Even though it was a mild winter, it was still cold, with frost covering the backyard grass. Paul was glad that he also had the attachment that turned the top of the kettle into a small stove-top, allowing someone to cook while at the same time heating water. He made sure to leave the spout open, as the rubber stopper attached to the kettle with a chain could become a projectile, as the water boiled. The water tended to boil in these kettles as fast as someone putting the same amount of water into a microwave oven, if not faster. Paul knew he would love this device.

Paul and Emily sat at the dining room table, drinking their respective coffee and tea. Mitten, Tiny Baby and Tigger all joined them, as if the cats were attending a family meeting. It was a little chilly in their well-insulated house, but still warmer than the outdoor temperature. Paul had thrown-on green sweatpants and one of his Marine Corps surplus fleece pullovers in coyote color, with thick, military-type sand-colored socks that Paul wore indoors. Emily was in her nightgown, robe and slippers. They talked about what they would prioritize. Tiny Baby jumped into Paul's lap. Mitten, ever the mama's boy jumped into Emily's lap. The elderly Tigger, who Paul now nicknamed Granny, sat on the floor between them all.

"Here in a minute, I'll go get the Big Berkey out of the attic. Until I get the rain barrels reconnected to our downspouts, we can use the water from the creek. I already filled our five gallon plastic water container for the Kelly Kettle this morning," Paul said. "We also need to get started on my idea for sanitation. Actually, that's going to be priority number two. I'm gonna to get started on that, next."

Paul continued, as he drank his coffee.
"In a few days, I'm gonna go ahead and re-deploy our little 12-gauge friends. I'll point them out to you once they're in place. Each area will be marked-off on our side with some metal minefield signs and 550 cord. I got the signs from a surplus dealer, on-line."

The signs Paul referred to were military-issued, red-colored triangular metal signs with the the word MINES printed on them. Paul had bought them years earlier. Back during the Cold War he had been trained in identifying minefield placards. They had holes punched in them from which they could be strung using any cord, or string.

After finishing his coffee, Paul grabbed the ladder he used earlier and retrieved the British Berkfeld water filter system from their attic, setting it up in the kitchen. He was now ready to work on his next project.

After doing some upper body stretching, Paul got busy. Using a pick ax and shovel to dig a hole in the far corner of their back yard, he dug as far from the creek, on the opposite side of their suburban property as possible. In the meantime, for any solid waste the plan was to use their regular toilets but with a five-gallon bucket, with which to flush them while the sewer system still functioned.

While Paul was doing this, Emily was pulling supplies out of their crawlspace and organizing them in their storage/laundry room, situated off the back of their garage. Ammunition in one area, stored food, hygiene and medical supplies in their respective areas.

* * *

Two days later, Paul's six-foot latrine hole was finished. He left excess dirt surrounding the edge of the hole, covering it with an old wooden pallet, then covering that with a sheet of heavy vapor barrier plastic. He weighted down the corners with large, round stones, and covered the edges with more dirt. This should keep the flies and small animals out, Paul thought. It was going to be a pain in the ass sealing this up each time he dumped their solid waste into it, but he let Emily be the boss this time.

Paul also realized that he was going to have to provide some overhead cover to keep the rain off of this patch of ground. One of his brown tarps and some OD green para-cord should do the trick, he thought.

Paul had originally wanted a real commercial porta-potty in this spot for the backyard, with a large hole cut into the bottom of it. He would probably have to come up with a used one now, after-the-fact. Since Paul had a knack for cleaning and restoring things, it should be no problem.

It was also now time for an outdoor shower. Years ago at a gun show, Paul had found an army surplus five-gallon field shower in excellent condition. It had cost him only ten dollars. Paul had felt like a little kid on Christmas morning, the day that he bought it.

Paul hung the field shower on the limb of their backyard butterfly shrub, not far from the latrine hole. The floor consisted of another wooden pallet and another brown-colored tarp, for privacy.

Paul also started setting up more of his small, milled aluminum .12 gauge friends. Their placement was prioritized on where a bad guy would likely try to infiltrate the property: over the top of the fence in certain locations, between shrubs where only someone sneaking onto the property would approach, etc.

* * *

On a chilly morning about a week later, Paul sat on the living room floor in front of a nice roaring fire in the wood stove with a cup of instant coffee. Tiny Baby was sitting like a sphinx on a nearby padded chair, facing the fire, enjoying its warmth. Emily was still in bed, as they were getting accustomed to being awake and alert at opposite times of each other.

The wood stove was a fireplace-insert design, its metal box extending out in-front of the original fireplace. It was a very efficient design for heating the entire living room. Having awakened about an hour earlier, Paul was thinking of what they had accomplished during the last few days. The Big Berkey was in the kitchen, doing its thing. The dry sanitation hole was dug. They now had a comfortable outdoor shower. Their backyard rain barrels were back in position, filling with rainwater as he sat there.

Suddenly Paul heard a knock on the door. Paul set his coffee on the coffee table in front of the leather sofa, then ran down the hallway into his study. From the window there, straining to look at an angle, he saw an unattractive dark-haired woman in her 40s with two children, a boy and a girl, both under 10 years of age. All had raincoats on, with hoods drawn.

Paul then headed for Emily's office, putting his OD green nylon pistol belt on. Damn. He hadn't removed the screens from the windows yet, in the event of having to throw lead, in the near future. Paul opened the window, which was the closest to the front door, just a crack, while remaining at an extreme angle, behind the brickwork of their house.

"Can I help you?"

"Hi, I'm the neighbor from across the street" she said, looking at what little she could see of Paul through the window. She gestured with her hands towards the north, behind her, indicating the houses across the street on the north side of the intersection that Paul and Emily lived on.

"My family's having hard times right now, with the stores

being out of stuff and everything, and I was wondering if you had any food you can spare. Just for my kids?"

Paul knew the house. It was immediately north of them, across the intersection, where it appeared that two families had already been living, under one roof. He felt sorry for the kids. They seemed pitiful in their hooded raincoats. However, he and Emily just did not have the resources to dispense charity for an event like this, where any near-term resolution seemed doubtful. Even if they chose to dispense charity under these circumstances, in this suburban setting, soon every neighbor who needed something would be knocking at their door.

"No, I'm sorry. We don't really have any food right now, either," Paul said in a quiet, raspy voice, as if tired or hungry, himself.

"OK, sorry to bother you," she said, turning away with a disappointed look on her face. Paul watched as the woman and her two kids headed across the street, towards Frank's house. He didn't need to watch anymore. However, he did start scanning for any sign of anyone accompanying her, either as an escort or someone observing from a distance as they tried to gauge their neighbors. He didn't see anyone from his limited vantage point.

About a week into this now and the neighbors are already looking for food, Paul thought to himself. He realized that he was going to need to be more convincing in the future, in responding to people coming to the door.

* * *

Three weeks into the collapse, and the overnight frosts seemed to have ended. It was now spring, and things were starting to grow again. Paul had replanted his raised beds in the back yard with above-ground plants such as romaine lettuce, spinach, and tomatoes. He also planted zucchini and potatoes, mainly as calorie crops. In the front yard, in the southern end where he grew stuff, he took a chance on planting more potatoes and romaine lettuce. Paul was worried about the perennials in the front yard, however: the kale and Swiss chard. Hopefully, the idiot neighbors would simply regard them as weeds or leftover decorative plants.

On that same thought, Paul wanted to re-research the weeds that grew around his planted crops. These naturally occurring plants, such as dandelion and common chickweed were not only edible but often more nutritious than what was actually planted. The one-inch blackberry vine shoots at this time of year were like multivitamin pills: All the nutrients that a baby shoot needs to grow into a large blackberry vine. He consulted his copy of *Pacific Northwest Foraging* by Douglas Deur for more info. Also, if worse came to worse, the grass in their front and back yards was edible as well.

That same grass was about a foot tall now, as mowing it was not just simply removed from the priority list, but would have been a dead giveaway of a maintained residence, as well as an obvious sign of abundant fuel storage.

Paul and Emily tried to stay off of their lawns as much as possible, so as not to make any noticeable tracks. Much of Paul's motivation for this came from the U.S. Army's old 1968 field manual, *Camouflage* (FM 5-20). Much of the field manual dealt with camouflaging positions from overhead imagery and imposing vehicular traffic discipline in rural areas. Paul made more of his indoor magic marker signs, reminding both he and Emily to stay off of the grass in both yards.

Paul also pulled out his backup electrical system out of the shed. It consisted of a PowerHub 1800 solar generator with an additional battery expansion unit. He liked this system, since it met his requirements for electrical generation: It used no fossil fuels to charge a bank of deep-cycle batteries. Instead, it used electricity generated from either solar panels, a wind generator, or another 120-volt AC source such as a generator, or simply plugging into an outlet (prior to an expected power outage, for example). It was portable, yet it could also be permanently grid-tied into the house.

Paul had three deep-cycle lead-acid batteries for this device that he kept stored with it. He had used the fourth one for his Dodge Diesel when it had needed a replacement battery. Paul knew that dry batteries stored better than batteries with electrolyte in them, but sometimes as a survivalist you couldn't let the perfect become the enemy of the good, in terms of getting your preps in order. However, he still needed to find a fourth large, deep-cycle lead-acid battery.

Paul was also aware of other long-life batteries, the type preferred by people living off-grid, such as nickel-iron batteries, an invention of Thomas Edison's, himself. These batteries were known to last for decades and actually improved with age. All one had to do was maintain the water level in these batteries. However, they produced less current than lead-acid batteries and were also prohibitively expensive. In addition, Paul wanted to put a system together sooner rather than later.

Paul had a 90-watt solar panel on its own two-wheeled frame, along with another set of three 15-watt panels he once bought from the Harbor Freight store chain. Although it offered more energy density, wind generation was out of the question. He would have to place the wind generator on a mast or other structure at least 20-feet off of the ground in order to receive a decent amount of wind-driven electrical power from it. It also would be a calling card to the rest of the neighborhood that someone in the area had electrical power.

The solar panels needed to stay tactical. Paul never even

entertained the thought of placing them on the south side of his roof for everyone to notice. Paul had to sacrifice some efficiency in order to keep the panels out of view. By simply having them in the backyard at ground level, he kept them concealed within his backyard fence while still angled upwards, toward the southern sky.

Having analyzed the wattage requirements of all of the appliances in the house, Paul concluded that he could use the solar generator to power any single 120 VAC device in the house: the refrigerator, dishwasher, clothes washer, garage door opener, etc, as long as it wasn't primarily used to generate heat (other than the coffee maker).

As Paul was getting their electricity established, Emily was working on blacking-out the house. All window blinds and drapes were kept closed. What spare blankets and comforters they had were duct-taped over the most obvious windows, so that no light would escape. As the weeks progressed they didn't want to advertise the fact that they had *some* electrical power, or to advertise that someone was actually living there. Paul also designated the storage/laundry room between their garage and their dining room as a *light lock*. Similar in principle to an air lock on a spacecraft or submarine except in this case interior light was being contained. The interior door to this room stayed closed at all times. It was also kept dark. Light coming from inside the house would never be exposed through this room as anyone entered or exited the room through its backyard door, or its door to the garage, if the garage door happened to be open. Paul also double-checked the blacked-out exterior of the house using his night vision monocular.

As the next few weeks passed, Paul and Emily stayed busy inventorying their food supply and creating an Excel-type product (actually Calc in Apache OpenOffice) on their netbook and laptop computers to record it all on, along with ammunition and medical supplies. They were also fine-tuning other preps, such as loading weapons magazines, conducting display layouts on the floor of various types of gear: Everything from tactical military-related items to body armor and related protective gear, electronic security, early warning systems, etc. The biggest challenge was gathering-up all of the separated items between the house and the backyard shed.

For entertainment in the evenings they would read. Paul usually brushed-up on how-to manuals, tactical skills, etc., either in hard copy or stored on his netbook. Emily usually read some of her Christian women's books, from her collection. They also kept the three cats entertained. Tiny Baby, in particular liked to chase a visible laser dot. They were all still total primadonnas: they had to be brushed with their separate brushes each evening. Tigger, or Granny, as Paul liked to call her (inspired by the old *Downton Abbey* TV series), was getting old. She used to resemble a fat little gray-striped snow tiger. Soon, she would need to be put-down. Paul was beginning to worry more-and-more about the cats going out in the evenings. He remembered the news from 2016, of the starvation in Venezuela devoiding the streets of cats, dogs, pigeons, etc. Even zoo animals were not spared.

They would also listen to one of Paul's shortwave receivers, a small, portable Grundig-brand receiver. At night, when the stations would come in they could hear fairly clear signals in various foreign languages. One trick that Paul used to get better reception was to use a test wire, with alligator clips at each end. One end would be clamped to the radio's antenna, the other to a larger metal structure, such as a window frame, or even the aluminum canopy of a pickup truck.

One station they were receiving was Radio Havana, in English. Radio Havana was a white propaganda news service aimed at the U.S., which always loved to remind Americans of the problems within their country. Radio Havana described among other things the list of American cities hit by nuclear warheads. They also mentioned that the U.S. was not appealing to any other countries for aid, at the moment.

* * *

As the sunny days followed by the rainy days of a typical Pacific Northwest spring continued, Paul did not see much community being formed in his neighborhood. He would see a couple of neighbors who already appeared to know each other talking, but that was about it. It appeared that no one trusted each other. Go figure. Before the collapse, Paul had been the only one who had actually showed up for the city neighborhood association meetings, besides the president, vice president, and a local police officer. Pretty sad, when the only one showing for the meetings was an admittedly somewhat reclusive survivalist.

Paul knew that having a local community was important in any long-term survival situation. As a professional survivalist however, he had always stressed that it depended on what you actually *had* for people living around you. In Paul and Emily's case, there was no community in their neighborhood. It was filled with clueless Umericans, or 'Merikins, as some societal critics and collapse theorists referred to them. Therefore, Paul and Emily needed to conceal their preps as much as possible.

Paul was mentored years earlier by fellow survivalists in the military, who told him that it was his job to go out there and form community: organize them, train them, etc. At one time, a like-minded Lieutenant Colonel he had once met at the US Army War College had stressed to him:
"You're a Lieutenant. That means you can run a platoon."

Great, Paul had thought. Everything that Paul had encountered or witnessed, from his abuse and abandonment as a child, the various personalities he encountered in the military, to the decline of American society, made him think otherwise. He really did not give a damn about any of his neighbors, most of whom had clearly not prepared for anything. What was the point of trying to create community with them, if they had nothing to offer? Paul had read people's accounts from Jim Rawles' *SurvivalBlog*, where neighbors in upper-middle class neighborhoods in particular would beg to borrow things during an emergency, such as during a blizzard, or extended power outage. These same people would not only have nothing to offer in return, but after the weather event, power outage, etc. would not even bother to return said items, and would not even bother to offer any kind of thanks when the prepared individual had to pay them a visit, in order to get their stuff back.

He did notice over recent years, though, how more of his neighbors were growing more of their own food. Even a neighbor on the other side of the creekbed who seemed to be an enabler for a house full of in-laws who were drug addicts, was growing corn and other food crops in her backyard.

For some reason, Paul was reminded of one of his favorite documentary films, the BBC documentary produced by filmmaker Adam Curtis, titled *Century of the Self*. This was a powerful documentary film, describing the conclusions Freud drew from his work in psychoanalysis, along with Freud's rascally-young nephew, Edward Bernays, who took his uncle's theories on primitive, uncontrollable human urges in order to convert World War I internal propaganda into something he called Public Relations.

Freud had concluded that human beings were an incredibly savage species, more so than any other mammal, and were capable of inconceivable brutality. While originally ridiculed for his theories, he was vindicated a few years later as World War I continued in its mass slaughter of hundreds of thousands in single battles. This was helped along by the advent of machine guns, flamethrowers, the use of poison gas, etc.

After Freud emigrated to England in the late 1930s in order to avoid getting caught up in the Nazi takeover of Austria, he simply shut himself off from the rest of society, regarding humanity as hopelessly irredeemable and simply too savage a species to deal with. Soon, his insights would be vindicated once again.

Paul had felt somewhat inspired by that Adam Curtis documentary, viewing American society in much the same way as Freud did society in general, in his day.

Bugging In

* * *

Whenever Paul went outside at night, in order to work in the garden or to go out to the backyard shed, as a minimum he always wore his Springfield Armory .45 cal. XD pistol on an OD green gun belt, in a Blackhawk quick-draw holster with an extra two-mag pouch on the opposite side.

Paul thought he would take a chance and go outside this particular morning. As he was examining his kale and Swiss chard plants, he noticed the 30-something guy who lived next to their neighbors across the street. The guy walked to the car in his driveway; he was about 20 yards away. They waved hi to each other.

Great, Paul thought. Paul once saw this neighbor at a large flea market, back when Paul used to have a lot of .50 BMG ammunition for sale. God I hope he doesn't come sniffing around, Paul thought. Just do the nerdy neighbor routine who doesn't know what's going on. Paul couldn't remember his name, if his life had depended on it. For some reason, this neighbor reminded Paul of the fabled CIA gray man: Not too short, not too tall, no particular hair color (light brown?). The kind of guy who could walk right past you, and you'd never notice him. Since the neighborhood had been pretty boring lately, Paul had tried to keep an eye on him, as well as on the rest of the neighborhood, without making it too obvious. Guys like him drove Paul up the wall. It reminded him of the scene from the movie *Tombstone,* when Doc Holliday confronts Johnny Ringo for the first time:

"I don't know... There's just something about him. Kind of reminds me of... Me... Now I truly hate him."

Of course, Paul didn't really hate this guy. Paul wondered where his hot, model-like little girlfriend, fiancé, or whatever-she-was, was. Paul had not seen her since the bombs fell. She was slim, somewhat short, with long light brown hair. Paul had recently seen the couple out for a walk together using sign language: apparently she was deaf.

How sad, Paul thought. Disabled people were going to be in the first wave of a die-off in the event of a fast crash, as he had mentioned to his consulting clients and readers.

When Paul was finished working weeds with a hula hoe, he noticed out of the corner of his eye that the same neighbor had just been sitting in his car, a blue Toyota sedan, with the door closed. Paul continued his weeding.

BOOM!

Suddenly, the inside of the driver side window of the neighbor's car was covered in blood, with a hole blown through it.

Emily ran out the front door into the yard. "What happened?" She had been looking out of her office window and had seen Paul looking at something across the street after hearing the gunshot.

Paul turned his head to Emily. "I think the neighbor just off'd himself."

Emily raised her hands to her mouth. "Oh my God."

It was the first time Paul actually ever heard her use the word God, instead of 'gosh,' or 'oh my goodness,' in that phrase.

"Yeah, we're gonna see more of that," Paul said, looking across the street, then back at Emily. He started thinking to himself. Come to think of it, many of those single gunshots he had heard in the neighborhood must have been suicides. He knew that the trend in suicide had skyrocketed in the US after 2008, and that by 2011, suicides had officially surpassed traffic accident fatalities each year, according the National Institutes of Health. He wasn't surprised by any of this.

"Shouldn't we go see if there's anyone else in the house? Someone just killed themselves. Maybe he shot someone else, too."

"Probably not a bad idea." He headed back inside the house.

Even if there was no one there who needed help, the house might hold some supplies that they could use.

In his study, Paul grabbed his OD green plate carrier and 1990's-era Kevlar helmet, which also had a riot control-looking, flip-down face shield attached to it. However in this case, the transparent shield was made of inch-thick material, rated to stop .12 gauge and .357 Magnum, on-down. He put on a pair of tactical knee pads in ACU green, elbow pads in coyote color and his main battle rifle. He also donned his Peltor 6-S headphones to be worn under the helmet. Wait: This is a house clearing deal. Paul put the 5.45mm M4 back and grabbed the Benelli M2 .12 gauge tactical shotgun instead. Although it only held five rounds of three-inch .12 gauge, it was a high-quality, elegantly made, reliable weapon. The M2 was the recoil-operated version of the US Military's M4 gas-operated .12 gauge shotgun. However, it still kicked like a mule when fired. Paul made sure to load it with .00 buck. He also grabbed a small OD green plastic US military chemical detector-kit box. This box had a flip-top lid with a shoulder strap attached. It was divided into two halves. In one half Paul stored 2-3/4-inch .12 gauge cartridges in .00 buck. The other side was filled with 2-3/4-inch rifled slugs. Slung across him on his opposite side, it made for quick reloading into the shotgun's tube magazine.

"Do you need any help?" Emily asked while Paul was putting on his gear. She was so sweet, Paul thought: Even though her only formal training had been with a handgun, she still offered to help.

"No, that's OK, sweetie. I think I'll be OK. Just keep an eye on things out here for me."

"OK."

Once Paul finished suiting up, he headed across the street. He turned the gain all the way up on the headphones for enhanced hearing. He walked past his neighbor's bloodied car, seeing the exit hole through the driver-side window, the inside of it draped in blood and brain fragments.

"OK, time to get serious," Paul said under his breath. Standing with his back to the house, off to the left side of the front door, he reached with his left hand and knocked on the door.

"Hello! Is anyone in there," he yelled out into the house.

There was no reply. Paul tried the doorknob. It was unlocked. With the shotgun's single-pane reflex sight turned-on, showing a red electronic cross-hair, he put the stock into his shoulder with his right eye behind the sight, both eyes open. Keeping his strong right leg behind him in a forward-leaning combat stance, he entered the house.

As he entered the living room of the house, looking left and right, keeping the .12 gauge pointing down the hallway of the house, he didn't see anything unusual. As he entered the kitchen, he saw a small white dry-erase board on the side of the refrigerator.

Where's Jennifer?

That must be Little Hot Stuff, Paul thought. He continued down the hallway, ready for someone to pop out of one of the bedrooms. He glanced into a side bedroom and saw a body lying on a bed, with a white sheet pulled over it.

Who the fuck is that, Paul thought. He remembered that this neighbor shared his house with his father. Let's see. Paul approached the bed, using the muzzle of the Benelli to lift the bed sheet from the face. A smell was already starting to set in.

"Damn... Yeah, that's Daddy," Paul said, as he winced, pulling his head away from the sight of decaying flesh. The smell, plus the sight, made Paul vomit without hesitation. Paul was sensitive to smells like people's bad breath, or for that matter, the rotten-meat smell of a dead mammal. For some reason at that split-second moment, Paul thought of the TV series from several years back, *The Walking Dead.* If the dead coming back to life could have been real, how could anyone have stood the non-stop smell, not to mention the diseases that would have been everywhere?

"Oh Jesus," he said aloud, wiping his mouth with the back of his hand, recovering from the involuntary action. Shit... Paul thought. What if someone just heard him? He went towards the door-frame, dropped to his knees, poking his helmeted and shielded head around the door frame. Looking in both directions, he didn't see anyone. Paul just remembered: This guy had a large dog. Where is it? He didn't hear or see the dog. He continued down the hallway to the master bedroom.

As he scanned the bedroom with the military-style .12 gauge on his shoulder, he didn't see anyone. He got on his knees, and checked under the bed. Nothing.

"Is there anyone in this house, Paul yelled-out. You need to come out *now*. I mean you no harm."

He heard nothing.

After waiting about a minute, he relaxed a little.

"OK. Time to go shopping," Paul said to himself. He went into the kitchen, going through the cupboards, looking for anything he and Emily could use. Plates, a nice glass set, mixed coffee cups were what greeted Paul. In one cupboard was a collection of prescription medicines, in various sizes of brown plastic containers. He couldn't recognize the names, except for one: An empty prescription bottle for Xanax. Paul knew that Xanax was a powerful anti-anxiety or anti-depression medication, which was potentially addictive.

Next he entered a closet off of the kitchen. There was a small bag of flour and a couple of boxes of baking soda. Paul grabbed these items, setting them on the floor near the front door.

Paul then headed for the entrance to the garage, tactically scanning it with the large automatic shotgun. Great. It was dark. Paul should have brought the PVS-14. As his eyes adjusted to the dim light coming from some translucent windows, Paul saw that the garage was filled with two vehicles: a large truck, and a sedan. It was also filled with a lot of junk: shelves full of tools, various motor oils, chemicals, etc. He also spotted a 20-pound bag of dog food.

"OK, this stuff could come in handy." Paul also found some five-quart jugs of motor oil in 10w30, and 5w30, along with some motor oil in 15w40: Diesel motor oil! He opened the caps to confirm. Yup. Foil-sealed spouts. Brand new!

Paul went back into the kitchen. He scooped up the meager stuff he found in their pantry. As he was heading back to his house he realized now why the guy had just offed himself: The love of his life had gone missing in all of this with God only knowing what had happened to her, along with the guy's dad dying. And, no food in the house.

However, other thoughts entered Paul's mind. As a collapse theorist, Paul had put forward a theory years earlier with other theorists, that in the event of a die-off of the human population in the US, there would actually be an overabundance of certain household items due to a sudden drop in the population: Everything from bed sheets, to kitchenware, to tools. However expendable items, such as paper and light plastic products, hygiene items, etc., would be very different in a long-term scenario, with little-to-no recovery.

This guy could have made other arrangements for himself, Paul thought. This early into this crash event, Paul was not prepared to dispense charity, but the guy could have traded with Paul, and Paul would have gladly traded some food items for the guy's other belongings. Granted, Paul would have gotten the better of the deal, and with no apologies. Paul was the guy who had prepped: This guy clearly hadn't, so it sucked to be him. The guy could have hooked up with a group, a neighbor, etc. Was there anyone in Paul and Emily's immediate neighborhood that was fairing any better? It was probably the Xanax. If he was taking that prescription drug and ran-out, go figure.

Paul returned to the guy's house, still armed, still tactically geared up, but this time wearing one of his large-sized, US military-issue ALICE packs. He headed back into the kitchen, grabbing any sugar, spices, salt, pepper, and other staples that he could find. It wasn't much. He stuffed these items into the outer pouches of the ALICE pack.

Next, Paul went back into the garage. Setting the shotgun against a wall, Paul loaded the 20-pound dry dog food bag into the ALICE pack. That'll make great back-up dry food for the cats, he thought.

He then loaded four of the five-quart oil jugs into the pack. He tried putting it on his back.

"Hello. Now it's a party," Paul said aloud as he struggled to first pick it up, putting it onto his right shoulder, then his left, cinching that side of the backpack tight. No matter how heavy the load, a good old ALICE pack always handled it well.

As he left the house, he noticed the bloodied car, once again. Why didn't I check his weapon for Christ's sake, he thought to himself. As Paul opened the car door, the body began to fall out of the car sideways, dumping more blood onto the driveway. Damn. He found the pistol on the floor under the steering wheel. It was a Beretta 92F, 9mm, in excellent condition.

"Nice."

Snuffy

* * *

"Back in my time, being crazy used to mean something. Nowadays, everybody's crazy."

> – Charles Manson, in a late 1980's interview with Geraldo Rivera

The Raven Rock Mountain Complex, also known as Site R or the Alternate Joint Communications Center, was nestled into the hills of southern Pennsylvania, just across the state border from Maryland. It was literally the Cheyenne Mountain bunker of the East Coast. The RRMC was a vast underground complex buried underneath one of the many unassuming hills of that region.

It was believed that during the 9/11 attacks, a vehicle convoy consisting of Vice President Dick Cheney and others had traveled to Site R, as part of a pre-planned Continuity of Government procedure.

However, in its normal role Site R served as the Continuity of Government site for The Pentagon. In the event of a national emergency, all essential military personnel who worked at The Pentagon were to be evacuated to Site R. From there, they would continue global operations. As instructed, the personnel who were tasked to evacuate directly from The Pentagon to Raven Rock even maintained their own bugout bags of personal items, stored in their offices, for this purpose.

"Well, here we are again," Senator Gregory Durham told the Joint Chiefs, sitting around him in a meeting room that resembled an elegant corporate setting: a large, elegant solid-wood meeting table, overhead accent lighting, etc. Except in this case, it was deep underground. He remembered being here during 9/11, standing in the rear of a group, being addressed by Vice President Cheney, whom he had idolized. He had never felt so alive as he did at that moment. He was itching for the Vice President to launch missiles. *Yes, do it*, Senator Durham had thought at that time.

Now it was even better. *He* was living the dream! People were going to be reminded once and for all of the power of the United States of America.

This was the third meeting Senator Durham was having with his joint Chiefs since they had arrived at Site R. He was smiling from ear-to-ear. "So, what's our status as of this point?"

The Army Chief spoke up. "Well, the DC area is still uninhabitable. We now estimate that it was hit by at least three thermonuclear warheads."

"Jesus," the Senator replied, almost laughing. "What about the other cities?"

"We can now confirm that New York, Boston, Baltimore, and Charleston have been wiped out, effectively taking out a good percentage of the US population along with them," the Army Chief said.

Boston. Now there's a real liberal town, the Senator thought.

The US Army Chief of Staff continued: "As for the West Coast, the entire Seattle area, along with all of the nearby military installations in that area have been wiped-out. San Diego and Los Angeles have also been hit."

"So what did we do to the Chinese," Senator Durham asked.

The Air Force Chief spoke next: "As I reported in previous meetings, every city with a population of over 100,000 throughout Mainland China has been hit by at least one 300 to 500 kiloton device. Unless everything important there went underground, The People's Republic of China no longer exists."

"Hell yeah," Senator Durham exclaimed, with a smile on his face that he was having a hard time controlling. He felt like a little kid in Disneyland. He wanted to yell out loud, "YEAH!" However, as difficult as it was, he couldn't reveal his true feelings around these men, even if they felt the same way.

"Alright, on to another subject: Security," the Senator said. "What do we have for perimeter defense?"

This ball went right back into the Army's ballpark. An Army Colonel addressed this question.

"As you know senator, we have a trained security force that has been drilled into reacting to a multitude of seizure-effort threats: Everything from protesters and militants to actual military assault. The problem is, with everything happening on short notice, and due to years of military downsizing, at this time we have no standing military units assigned to defend the perimeter of the site. All our support was to come from Fort Drum. As you know sir, Fort Drum was one of the military installations targeted by the Chinese. And since there were no combat arms units based there to begin with, we have no dedicated infantry units for conducting patrols, or for gauging the human terrain of the area around us, post-nuclear strike, in particular."

"You've got to be kidding me. Did someone actually plan it this way, or is this just the usual military planning, like the old Walter Reed scandal," the senator asked the group.

"Sir, these events happened so quickly, our entire military was caught off-guard, literally."

"Great. Do we at least have any air assets?"

"Most of our airbases were hit, the Air Force Chief replied. The only tactical aircraft we have left are the ones we redeployed to the Pacific to attack any remaining Chinese assets. And they're having maintenance and sustainability issues, as we speak."

"Oh, great. So much for downsizing and efficiency," the Senator said. He had been a critic of the Army and Air Force's Joint Base concept, turning Army posts and their adjoining Air Force bases into one giant military installation, not to mention all of the previous base closures. All it accomplished was making nuclear targeting that much easier for any adversary.

"Oh well. Lunch-time."

Bugging In

* * *

One Month After the Attack

The couples and small groups of people with children going door-to-door looking for food was getting worse.

Paul recognized none of the people who appeared almost daily now, on the color LCD monitor of his wireless LOREX camera. It was positioned on the ground along the front of the house, facing the side of the small cement front step. Paul was also able to see some of the northeast side of their yard through the camera, which was normally a blind spot, that could not be seen from any window. The camera was camouflaged, first with a base coat of flat brown spray paint, then some spray-on adhesive, then dirt, leaves, etc. Its power cord, and the green extension cord that it was connected to, were buried under dirt and old decorative bark. It was protected from the rain by the overhang of their house's roof. It was now getting its power from a deep-cycle marine battery, rotated among the others from his PowerHub 1800 charging system.

Paul knew from the writings of other professional survivalists that you never open the front door even a crack for anyone, period, in a WROL, or Without Rule of Law scenario. A seemingly innocent woman or an individual child could come to the door, while a sniper from a concealed position sat 100 yards away, ready to do a head-shot on the person opening the door. And this was just one of many possible strategies someone could use to force their way into someone's home, once the front door had been opened, even by so much as a crack. Therefore, the front door stayed shut at all times. As a rule, they now accessed their front yard by going into the backyard, and out through the side-gates of their six-foot, wooden fence. Paul had even taped another one of his Magic Marker reminder messages on the inside of the front door:

KEEP DOOR
SHUT AT
ALL TIMES !!!

In addition, Paul had placed some military OD green duct tape across the doorknob as a reminder, in the event of a morning without coffee.

Paul and Emily had set up a routine in the event that people came to the door. They would normally not answer it. If it was a group with men in it, in particular who started looking around when no one came to the door, he or Emily would go ahead and answer them by opening the window in Paul's study, sliding it open by just a crack rather than opening the front door. Paul and Emily kept a small plastic container of wood stove ash ready near the window to rub into their faces, giving an unhealthy color to their skin. Paul and Emily could have addressed them through the intercom built into the camera system itself, but that was out of the question, for obvious reasons.

He was guessing that many of the people were from outside the immediate neighborhood. Go figure. With the way Ridgefield, Washington had been developed by the usual parasites, it created more population density, the sworn enemy of a survivalist. Those assholes knew that the only way to sell real estate in the new economic paradigm was to buy out anyone who sat on one or two acres, then develop it with low-cost housing, usually ticky-tack, minimally-built town houses of vinyl and plywood, all attached to each other.

It was ironic. Paul and Emily thought that by buying their home here almost two decades ago that the development would be limited. It turned out that events made them wrong, with all the farmland around them sold off to the parasitic developers over the years.

Although the house was paid for and they were debt-free, he and Emily had had no money, or time for that matter, to find a more remote home. Paul was not a fan of the bugging-out concept, anyway. His plan for a quick societal collapse had always been to hide in plain sight, for as long as possible, where their supplies, security, and food-growing operations were already in place, and have a Plan B, C and D, if necessary.

Over the years, the bugging-out concept had been way over-hyped, as far as Paul was concerned. Bug-out out to where? To voluntarily become a refugee? Even strategic bugging out, also known as Strategic Relocating, had its own issues, as far as self-fulfilling prophecies were concerned. Modern homesteaders' houses had burnt down due to accidents, along with other mishaps occurring. Before the nuclear attack, criminals were already casing rural properties in Washington State, due to the lack of neighbors in a given area. In addition, climate change-induced droughts, landslides, and forest fires had been wreaking havoc throughout the Pacific Northwest for years, now.

Paul and Emily's Plan B was the local preparedness group, north of them in Washington State, that they had trained with on-and-off, prior to the attack. However, their training had been centered around a potential bugout to some rural land held in long-term lease by two of its members. The group's training had focused on convoys, occupying an assembly area and classic infantry tactics, in a rural setting. Paul had been very concerned about the long-term sustainability of this plan, however, and had stressed the need for food foresting, and other concepts related to the practice of Permaculture. And, it would have to be done on a large scale for a quickly put-together group of possibly as many as 50 people, to include the elderly, children, and other less-capable people. The old retired Army Sergeant Major who ran the group had a couple of adult children of his own, still living at home, with their own issues. Mental illness being one of them.

Paul's plan regarding this group was to travel out to the group's retreat area and check on their status, but to do it carefully. His plan was to camouflage whatever vehicle he had used to get there, shoot a compass azimuth and approach the rest of the way on foot. What if his worst fears for them had been realized, and they had become reduced to a group of starving, yet heavily-armed refugees? Although they were his friends, if hungry enough, they could jack him and try to force out of him the exact location of his home and supplies. It was literally unthinkable. They were his friends, but Paul knew that a group of starving people were capable of anything.

* * *

It was a pleasant sunny spring morning when a small group of people came looking for handouts. The group consisted of four adults who appeared to be two separate couples and three children, one about 12 and the other two younger, between eight and 10 years of age. The adults appeared to be in their 40s. One could tell that the women had lost weight, although they still appeared overweight and unattractive.

Emily opened the window in Paul's study to address them. She held their Benelli M2 semi-automatic shotgun at the ready, out of view.

"I'm sorry, but we don't have anything ourselves," she said in a quiet voice to them, while keeping her head and face inside the window, out of view, and behind the house's brickwork.

"Bullshit," the oldest 40-something man of the group said. He had dark features with dark, unkempt hair. "We've walked around here before and you people have never left your house, *at all*. Look. Our kids are starving. We just want you to share *something*, for Christ's sake!"

Emily knew from prior conversations with Paul that opening the door for any reason was a death warrant for them. Without saying anything to them, she walked quickly to their bedroom.

"Paul... Paul," she yelled, shaking him. He was in bed asleep, having just come off of his night-time and early morning 12-hour shift and had only been asleep for roughly two hours.

"What."

"There's a group at the door, and they won't leave."

"Shit." He was pissed, and this particular morning would be no exception. He got out of bed, dead tired, not bothering to put anything over his brown military-issue briefs and OD green T-shirt. He donned his noise-canceling headphones, turning the sound amplifiers all-the-way up on each side and grabbing his OD green M4 rifle. Paul and Emily heard a couple of loud thuds at the front door. Paul worked the charging handle on the rifle as he entered his study.

The man who had been addressing Emily had just managed to pull-open the locked storm door, and was using his shoulder against their all-metal, white-colored front door.

"Watch the back of the house while I deal with these clowns," Paul told Emily. He then got into the same position that Emily had been in when she had addressed the group. With his rifle raised to his right shoulder, he looked at them through the tubular red-dot sight on top of his weapon. "Get the fuck out of here. You've got two seconds."

"Hey, we just want -"

BOOM! The older dark-haired man's head exploded as he fell straight down, like a suddenly-dropped large sack of potatoes. His head had been split down the middle like a character out of an old cartoon. Blood and brain fragments were sprayed onto the front of the house, and onto the group of people he had been with. The two women suddenly screamed in a short burst, bringing their hands to their faces as they stepped back. Even Paul was surprised by the mess created by the Soviet military-surplus 5.45 mm round.

"Yeah, anybody else want to push this? I said get the fuck outa' here," Paul said to the remaining group of people. Paul suddenly felt his heart beating loudly in his chest. He was right here. He was defending his home, and everyone in it. He was in his environment.

"You think you're somebody with that gun, don't you," one of the women screamed at Paul.

"No, just somebody who saw this coming, Honey. It's time for you NFL NASCAR idiots to get the fuck out of here,"

The children simply stood there in shock, looking at the dead body. They had seen it before, after all, in their computer games, just not for real and up close like this. The women were still crying. The other man, staring at his buddy's lifeless corpse, was crying as well and shaking his head back and forth. He looked at Paul with a strained look on his face. "Fuck you... Fuck you...,"

"OK, now that got that settled, how about taking what's left of your buddy, and getting the hell out of here," Paul said to the group. He didn't like swearing in front of children like this, but he needed the verbal effect that came from his anger at these people. And they were the ones who brought their kids to this, after all.

The remaining man, and one of the women, all still crying and saying their Oh my God's, grabbed the bloodied corpse with its mutilated head by the arms, dragging it off of the front step, more blood spilling on the walkway, heading back the way they came.

* * *

Paul had a pretty good idea that they would simply leave the body somewhere on their way home, lacking the energy to take it all the way back to wherever they came from. This time Paul was dressed: Solid OD green BDU trousers with matching T-shirt, old-school black combat boots, OD green plate carrier and Kevlar helmet with face shield. Paul entered the backyard with their Benelli M2 .12 gauge. He opened the padlocked, wooden-fenced gate on the north side of the property, entering the side yard. Through part of a hedgerow of solid blackberry, Paul saw where the body lay, face-up, arms extended, as if someone were preparing him to be crucified.

Paul then saw the remaining three adults and their kids heading away, down the road to the west, about 200 yards away. Paul looked around, not seeing any of the neighbors outside of their homes.

He then went about checking the guy's pockets. A Dennis Wilkins, address matching one of the newer neighborhoods, west of theirs. Probably one of those newer townhouses. Paul then came up with an idea.

He grabbed the body from behind, under it's arms, dragging it to the stop sign, on the corner of his property. Paul then propped the body sitting up, legs in front of it, facing into the middle of the intersection.

He went into the house, grabbing some OD Green 550 cord, a sheet of cardboard out of the garage, a magic marker pen, and his Gerber multi-tool. He then came out of the house with his new sign.

Paul then punched holes near the top corners of the cardboard. Wait: I can't believe I'm wasting an entire length of 550 cord on this project, he thought to himself. He then took the length of cord apart, pulling the white inner-strand material out of the OD green-colored cord. Paul knew that each of the seven inner-strands had roughly 35 pounds of tensile strength.

With the body sitting up and the blown-apart head facing down, Paul hung the sign around its neck, with the sign positioned on the man's chest.

I PICKED THE
WRONG HOUSE
TO FUCK WITH

Perfect.

* * *

When they got back to Marcia's house, the three remaining adults were talking among themselves.

"Oh my God, I can't believe that guy killed Dennis," Marcia said. He was her husband. Her neighbor couple, and all their children were still alive, at least. They had not been able to drag her husbands' corpse all the way home, so they left it on the blind side of that house they had been at. Maybe they could go back for it later. Bob was too weak to carry it. Some man, she thought.

She couldn't blame him, though. They were all starving. She just thought that any man could throw his buddy on his shoulders, just like in the movies. Even if there was a massive amount of blood coming out of a dead body.

Maybe that guy at his house had been right. Did we really live stupid lives, while some people, like that guy back there, knew more about what was going on in the world and prepared for it? I bet he could carry another man on his shoulders. He was probably physically fit and knew how to protect his house and his wife. Lucky woman. What did I get, even when Dennis *was* alive? A child, and someone who liked to get drunk, loud, and violent during Seattle Seahawks games. It felt stupid, the way he made us all walk around in public, wearing those Seattle Seahawks jerseys.

Linda, her friend who had accompanied her, along with her husband, interrupted Marcia's thoughts. "Hey, my 'ex in La Center used to have a couple of guns. Maybe we could go back and visit that son-of-a-bitch."

"Which one," the newly widowed woman asked, confused, through her tears.

"Both of them. We see if we can talk to my ex-husband, and maybe he'll help us go back to that house, and get them back for what they did to Dennis. Maybe we could make a deal with him for their stuff, after we take those people out."

Her husband didn't seem to like the idea. "I don't know. That guy back there seemed to be one of those take-charge types, like he was in the military, or something. Maybe one of those *Doomsday Prepper* types. Besides, I don't want to have to deal with your ex again."

"OK, we'll do it," Marcia, said.

"Maybe they have some food," her disheveled-looking 12 year-old said. He was hungry all the time, thinking more of that than his dead father. The handouts of food they had received, as much as his mom had tried to stretch them, were just not enough. As things had gotten worse, he didn't really miss his Dad much at this point, anyway.

"I guess we can use the fuel we've got left to go visit your ex," Bob said, reluctantly. I don't know if we'll have enough to get back, though."

"Sounds good to me," the widow said. "Johnny, why don't you stay with the other kids, and keep an eye on them. We'll probably be back, before too long."

"OK Mom."

* * *

They drove the widow's beat-up late-2000s blue Nissan sedan out to an old whitewashed clapboard house on some property that was obviously grandfathered, sitting in a commercial zone, with a small auto shop on one side and a tattoo parlor on the other. It was basically a dump.

The still-married woman's gray-haired ex-husband came out of the house, stepping onto an old creaky wooden porch with a couple of his friends. All were in their late 40s, all wearing a ball cap of some sort. All were in dirty clothes and unshaven. They all seemed to have lost weight since she had last seen them, but still appeared to be a bunch of slouches.

"Well, look who's here! The woman who said she was never going to have anything to do with me ever again," her ex-husband said.

"Hi Tom. Can you help us? Marcia's husband just got killed. All we were doing was asking for some food, and this guy killed him. You've got guns. Can you help us? There's probably a lot of stuff there for all of us."

Her ex-husband just looked down at her from the porch, and laughed. "Oh, you mean the old pump-action 12 gauge, and the old hunting rifle? The ones I have maybe a handful of bullets for, if I'm lucky? Besides, you said you weren't 'gonna have anything to do with me ever again, remember?"

"Oh my God, are you serious?"

:'M hum. So, what's your cute-looking friend's name again?"

"Marcia," Linda said.

"Hi Marcia... I think I have an idea." As he turned to head back into the house, he muttered to one of his friends. "This is too good to be true. You got your pistol on you?"

"Yeah."

The ex-husband came out of the house with an old, rusty long-barreled wooden-stocked shotgun. And with that unmistakable sound, jacking the slide, loading a round into the chamber, aiming it at Bob.

"OK, how about we do it like this: How about both you gals stay here at the house with us, and... What's your name?"

"Bob."

"OK Bob, why don't you take a hike... Wait a second, yeah. Why don't you leave your car here, and... Take a hike. The girls here can stay here with us," Tom said, as his two buddies, one on each side of him pulled away their shirts, revealing automatic pistols tucked in their pants.

"WHAT," both women exclaimed.

"I thought you were going to help us," Marcia said.

"Wait a second, that's my wife," Bob said.

"Not anymore. You know, I kind of like this end-o'-the-world shit."

"You can't just take someone else's wife," Bob said.

"You want to get your asses blown away? I can do whatever the fuck I want," Tom wasn't lying about hardly having any ammo, but he did have *some* and Bob here didn't seem like much of a problem, anyway.

Bob simply raised his hands.
His wife turned to him.

"I'll be alright."

"You can't just go with him!"

"I don't even know you," Marcia said to her friend's ex-husband.

"How about if you don't shut the fuck up, I blow your heads off. Now 'git walkin'," the ex said, gesturing back towards Bob.

Bob simply started walking backwards, then turned around, and continued walking back in the direction they had come from, tears coming from his eyes.

The two women simply stood there, watching Bob walk back towards the road.

"Party time you guys," Tom said to his buddies.

* * *

The decades-old grange building sat off to the side of an old county road in southern Pennsylvania, surrounded by fallow fields. The road had been turned back into gravel in recent years due to the lack of revenues to maintain the original paved road. At least the locals had been lucky enough to get the county to do that, before it went bankrupt.

"Do you think we can pull this off," the leader of a pre-nuclear attack preparedness group asked his peers. They all sat alongside each other. The speaker was just one of several older men sitting in a row of chairs on a short wooden stage in the old grange hall, facing their respective groups in the audience on the floor, below. Virtually everyone, particularly the small groups that now declared themselves as militias, wore some sort of military clothing or hunting outfits in RealTree pattern. Most wore a military tactical or hunter's vest, along with a rifle. There were many M4s, AR15s, AK's and a few larger military rifles in 7.62 NATO (308).

"I don't see why not. The federal government is just a paper tiger, anyway. Especially after the nuclear attack," one of the citizen's militia leaders replied. As of now, there are no standing military units assigned to the place, much less even patrolling its perimeter, he added.

"Wait a second, we didn't sign up for stuff like this," someone spoke out from the audience. She was an older, gray-haired woman from one of the smaller preparedness groups.

A different militia leader spoke up this time. "You signed up for this stuff when you became a prepper. Or excuse me, the proper term is survivalist."

"Yeah, but what are we trying to accomplish here? What's our end state? If we can't get access to site R, *then what*," another person from the audience asked.

"Then we pour some gasoline, and maybe even some good old home-made napalm, down their air vents," one of the more charismatic, though not very tactically competent militia leaders said. He continued. "We need to remember. In the first place, these are some of the latest assholes who led us up to this point. Even all the high-ranking military people there. Do you really think there's an Eisenhower or Patton in the bunch? These yes-men will turn on the American people in a heartbeat. They were all involved in the latest round of illegal wars, along with supporting ISIS and trying to pick a fight with Russia over Syria, just because the Russians were the only ones willing to do anything about ISIS. Do you really think they'll just quit their jobs when they suspend The Constitution? And they'll probably have even worse plans for those of us who prepared. Confiscating our larders, maybe even rounding us up for some of their FEMA camps. Stuff like that."

"We don't even know if all that FEMA camp stuff was for real. That was just shit we used to see all the time on the internet," another older female member of the audience said.

As a bunch of small conversations began taking place among the seated crowd of mostly middle-aged and heavily armed people, another member of the audience spoke up, addressing the panel of leaders. "Yeah, that's real smart. Do you have any idea how huge Raven Rock is? You may as well be trying to burn the people out of Cheyenne Mountain. Besides, if they know we're trying to gain access to the facility, who's to say they won't deliver one of their own remaining nukes right on top of their own site? We all know it's designed to withstand that,"

"It doesn't matter. If they don't have enough of their own supplies down there, then they're going to tax us for them, eventually. We have to do something," another member of the audience, dressed in Army ACU's with a tactical vest, said.

"We can pull this off if we operate within the limits of our capabilities," another leader of a small preparedness group said. He was sitting in the audience. His name was Randy, a local farmer, younger than the rest. He was in his early forties and a former U.S. Army Infantry Captain who had done tours in Afghanistan years earlier. He had been a gifted infantry officer, with a real feel for the game. If there had not been a massive draw-down of the U.S. Military, he would have had a stunning career.

However, along with that intellect came a conscience: He didn't like being the bad guy, in what he later discovered through research on the internet was a military invasion and occupation that had nothing to do with 9/11. It had all been based on failed negotiations with the Taliban *within the U.S.*, over an oil pipeline *before* 9/11. Much less did he feel fulfilled working his ass off in those "Provincial Reconstruction Teams," which the troops soon started referring to as "democracy-in-a-box." This push by the U.S. on self-sustaining tribal communities, who had lived their own way for centuries was ridiculous. It also reminded him of pacification efforts during the Vietnam War that he had read about. Same thing, using different titles. If anything, he had admired those people for the way they lived. It seemed like a formula for success: If you were self-reliant and could live off of the land, the U.S. couldn't defeat you.

"Yeah," several people from the audience said in unison.
"Right on," the younger people from Randy's group commented.
"That's easy for you to say," one of the people from another preparedness group said. "Most of us are in our 60's and 70's."
"Yes, that's true. But let me ask everybody here something. How many here are bench shooters, who shoot regularly," Randy asked.

At least half the room raised their hands.
"On that note, how many have .338 Lapuas, .308's, or .50 BMG rifles," Randy asked.

Of the men who had raised their hands, only half of that group put their hands back down.
"Wow," the former infantry captain commented, as he scanned the audience. It was more than even he had expected. His adrenaline was already going.

Standing from his chair, Randy addressed the crowd. "Okay, everybody take a look at these guys. No matter how old or slow these guys are, every one of them is what we call a force multiplier."

The last group of elderly men, as they lowered their hands, feeling complimented and the younger militia members in Randy's group all exchanged looks and nods of approval, showing solidarity to one another. The younger militia leader was feeling it too. This was what they called *unity of effort* when he went through his infantry training, and it was also a powerful component of asymmetric warfare. During his last tour in Afghanistan, there really had been no unity of effort between the Afghan National Army and his unit, which had been training them. He knew from his own experience that the side that had it usually won, even if at great cost.

* * *

Paul realized that it was now time to get more aggressive with the perimeter defense of the house. The gloves were coming off, literally, whether passers-by noticed it, or not.

If Paul remembered anything from the military, it was the three basic uses of obstacles:

- To block
- To delay
- To canalize, meaning basically to force or direct an enemy into an area where you want them. Useful also when obstacle-building materials are limited.

Gaps between the spruce tree and a couple of large shrubs on the north side of the property had already been filled-in with fertilized blackberry years ago, forming a spruce tree/shrub/blackberry hedgerow. However, people could still walk through it, if they were wearing heavy enough clothing, particularly any outer-layer of clothing consisting of nylon and/or GOR-TEX. They could also simply go around all of this and into the northern side of the front yard, a large rectangular space, where he had previously parked his large Dodge diesel. At the end of this was the north-side gate to the backyard, which faced east. At least anyone approaching from the street would be canalized, as they headed towards that particular backyard gate. Paul really wanted to fill in this rectangular area with some good old by-the-book, military tanglefoot. He just happened to have a 100-foot bobbin of barbed wire, courtesy of The Home Depot.

After driving some cut wooden stakes into the ground in random locations, Paul began stringing the barbed wire. He also wrapped the barbed wire several times around the bottom of the spruce tree itself, running it to the various posts, and to nails he positioned in the fence. While having fun being creative, Paul strung the barbed wire from nine inches to just over three feet off of the ground, criss-crossing it back over itself numerous times.

Perfect. His original blackberry-and-spruce-tree barrier along the street would canalize anyone toward the tanglefoot, where they would either be blocked again, or slowed down considerably, depending on the threat. Paul also rigged three of his .12 gauge Claymores inside of the tanglefoot, with two near the exterior wall of his garage in case someone tried to squeeze in between the wall and the barbed wire. Thanks to the awning pulleys that also had swivels built into them, Paul was able to position these facing up into the air, at an angle, towards the individual tripping the wire. All of the .12 gauge booby traps were spray-painted flat brown, then sprayed with an aerosol can of auto upholsterer's adhesive. Then dirt and leaves were thrown onto the traps, making the devices at each end of the tripwire invisible. In addition, weeds and grass would continue to grow in this area, obscuring the entire barbed wire/ tanglefoot construction.

Paul then went into the backyard and nailed one of his military-surplus MINES signs to the back gate, just as an extra precaution. As of now, no one could open the gate all the way anyway, with the tanglefoot in the way. Again, if the bad guys noticed any of his warning signs, it was better than the extreme alternative happening.

Paul then started working on their back yard wooden deck that the sliding glass door in their dining room opened onto. Paul stretched four of his 15-inch diameter razor wire spools around the entire outside of the deck. Using four strands, Paul nailed them to the wooden beams, bending them around the corners like a bunch of giant horizontally-mounted slinky toys. He then nailed the ends of the razor wire to the house's exterior siding. This effectively sealed off the deck from anyone entering or exiting it. Paul and Emily could still enter the back yard from the laundry room, which already served as the nighttime light-lock.

While Paul was doing all this, Emily was loading both of their pickup trucks with their supplies. Both were now backed up completely inside the two-car garage. It was tight, but with both trucks backed up to the house door, loading them was convenient and made them secure from observation. Paul felt lucky that they had already conducted this type of military-inspired load-out training with their local preparedness group. In the event of a good old survivalist-type bug out, Emily would be driving the larger ¾-ton, flat coyote-colored Dodge diesel. Paul would drive the smaller '95 Nissan pickup. Emily had never learned to drive a manual transmission, and it was unlikely that under the current circumstances he could teach her now. The Dodge had been well tuned and upgraded over the years, being Paul's favorite preparedness project. For Emily, it wouldn't feel much different from any fuel-injected, gasoline-fueled vehicle that she had ever driven.

Emily would just need to remember that it was diesel-fueled in the event that anything happened to Paul. He had reminded her that she could also use other fluids for fuel, such as automatic transmission fluid, motor oil, and vegetable oil, if added to regular diesel fuel. They also had a Bluegrass Systems 15-gallon fuel system for mixing and filtering used automatic transmission fluid, motor oil, or vegetable oil. The system included a 12-volt pump that connected to the truck's battery. Paul had once tried recycling used motor oil as fuel, but even this blended and filtered mix with regular diesel fuel seemed to pollute the engine. It created a nonflammable buildup somewhere between the engine and the exhaust, causing excessive smoke out of the tailpipe. It then took several tanks of regular diesel to clean the engine out. Used automatic transmission fluid, however, seemed to work somewhat better as an alternative fuel in the mechanically-injected Cummins turbo diesel engine. Needless to say, if an emergency occurred while on the road and fresh, unused versions of these alternative fuels were found, it would be that much better.

As Paul and Emily planned it out, each vehicle would be like a backpack on steroids specific to them, separately, in the event that one of them didn't make it to wherever they were going. Emily's clothing, for instance, would all be in her vehicle, along with all of the 9mm ammo for her Glock and it's carbine conversion. She would also pack half of all the 5.56 NATO, for the CAR-15, that

Paul had given her.

Paul's smaller Nissan pickup would load all of his clothing, along with his .50 BMG Armalite AR-50 rifle and all of its ammunition, and all of the .45 ACP ammunition. Since he was also the only one who shot 5.45x39mm, that ammunition all went with him. They divided the food larder between both vehicles. Paul's earlier reinforcement of the rear suspension of the little four-cylinder Nissan with air shocks, enabling a much heavier load in the bed was going to pay for itself. Both canopies, the cab-high fiberglass one on the Nissan and the cab-high aluminum one on the Dodge had good waterproof seals between themselves and the rails around each bed. Both canopies also had windowless sides, helping keep their contents hidden from nosy passers-by, any authorities, etc.

The first thing loaded into each vehicle was their ammunition, in-bulk, then their bulk food storage, along with bulk hygiene items. Everything was packed from floor to ceiling of the cab-high canopies in each truck. The last items loaded were items likely to be used in the short term, such as regularly worn clothing, loaded weapons magazines, and room for extra fuel storage. Paul normally didn't store fuel and ammunition together in the same space, but under the circumstances, it couldn't be helped. Important documents and hard family photos were also loaded into the cab of each truck. They had already kept all of their important documents in two Fat-50 ammunition cans.

They also packed traditional bugout bags. They consisted of two large Army surplus ALICE packs with aluminum frames. Each bag was basically a micro-version of what was already packed inside of each truck: Food, clothing, ammunition, and hygiene supplies. In Emily's case, she would also be using a two-wheeled, folding tourist's luggage cart, since she had no backpacking experience and didn't feel strong enough to wear a heavy backpack for any length of time. Each bugout bag was placed on the passenger seat for quick grab-and-go access in the event of an emergency, such as an ambush. This, Paul had learned from Jim Rawles' groundbreaking survivalist novel and instructional book, *Patriots*.

* * *

On the grounds of Site R in a guard shack outside of the underground complex and just inside the cyclone-fenced area, the two civilian black-uniformed Department of Defense guards were bored.

"Man, this sucks," one of the guards said, pushing his black baseball-style hat farther back on his head. "They're all safe down there, and we're up here, probably being exposed to all kinds shit."

"Yeah, you got that right," the other guard said. There's nothing out here, just some small farms and-"

SMACK. A red shower splat on the window behind the DOD guard's head and shattered glass, as his body dropped like a rock, followed by a distant rifle report. Other shots entered the guard shack, aimed at that same body

The other guard's eyes widened as he looked off into the distance to see where the shots came from. Several bullets entered his chest and abdomen, exploding out of his back in another bloody shower.

At that moment, camo-painted quad runners appeared in the distance across some farmland, making a direct run for the cyclone fence gate. As they approached the gate, they could already hear an alarm sounding-off in front of them, a constant monotone alarm, like something you would actually expect to hear from a nuclear bunker. It didn't deter the attackers, however.

As the quads approached the gate, heavily-armed men with rifles slung across their backs jumped off of them with metal-cutting saws and bolt cutters. Sparks flew as other local men on the other quads, all heavily armed, tactical vests loaded with magazines, began arriving and jumping from their vehicles. Once their work was finished, they entered the roadway which circled the large, grassy hill of Site R.

They headed directly for the parking area, where the various military and civilian DOD employees parked their vehicles. Jumping off again, this time with cordless power drills and fuel containers, they headed for the rear ends of the cars parked there.

In the hillside of Site R, roughly 100 yards away, an opening appeared: Sod was being lifted vertically out of the way to reveal the multiple barrels of a 7.62mm NATO, General Electric M-134 minigun. Suddenly, a sound like a fat man exhaling a single loud burp came from the 20th century version of the old Gatling gun.

The solid stream of bullets mixed with tracers swept the attackers like a garden hose, spraying blood, fuel, and fire as the fuel tanks on the quads and parked vehicles were ripped apart, the tracers detonating them. There was no time for the attackers to react. Some began to run for cover, as they were literally cut in half by dozens of rounds per body. The fire from the minigun ran only for a period of about seven seconds. The small fires from the vehicles spread to the rest of the automobiles parked there, bursting here-and-there in balls of flame.

Suddenly a volley of highly accurate fire was hitting the minigun, effectively disabling it. Bullets ranging from .308 Winchester to . 50 BMG were impacting the minigun, penetrating its mechanism, damaging its several barrels.

Permanent damage had now been rendered to both sides: The small assault element of the attack had been completely wiped out, with damage being done to Site R's perimeter.

* * *

After roughly a week, Paul decided to finally do something about the corpse he had left on the corner of his suburban property. It had been chewed on quite a bit by an assortment of feral dogs, raccoons, and scavenging rodents. After removing some of the bugout supplies from his truck, Paul lined the bed of his 1990's Nissan pickup with thick vapor-barrier plastic. Then, waiting until nighttime, wearing his latex gloves and Finnish military surplus gas mask, Paul dragged, then lifted and pushed the rotting, half-eaten corpse into the truck. He then drove to a nearby wilderness area underneath some power lines. Using a pickax and shovel, Paul dug a shallow grave, threw the corpse in the hole, and buried it.

The next morning, towards the end of his shift, while sitting on the living room sofa with a cup of coffee, he was still thinking of this incident. Years of mental preparation had prepared him for this after all, but it didn't mean that your nerves recovered from it, even after the fact.

Paul decided to let Emily sleep-in for a few hours, since he wasn't as tired as he usually was, after a 12-hour shift.

Suddenly, the LOREX camera monitor in Paul's study alarmed at something crossing in front of the house. Paul went down the hallway to check it out. Lifting the closed mini-blinds a tiny bit in his study, he saw a flat-sand colored, up-armored HMMWV pull in front of the house, coming to a stop just past the yard, in front of the opening to the creek bed, next to the house. Stenciled in black in two lines on the front passenger side door were the words HOMELAND SECURITY.

OK, Paul thought. "Emily! We got visitors," he yelled. Paul grabbed Emily's BDU-era Kevlar helmet and coyote-colored plate carrier. He also grabbed her Glock 17 carbine conversion with two loaded 31-round extended magazines. She bumped into Paul just as he was exiting his study. Paul handed her her gear.

"Watch the rear of the house. Lock and load. This is live. Anybody coming into view, waste them," Paul told her.

"Oh my God. OK."

Paul went back to the window in his study. He saw only two men come out of the HMMWV. There didn't seem to be anyone else in the vehicle. How'd they manage to come to his house without being ambushed by anyone, he thought to himself. Surely someone would have at least put a round into the side of their Humvee, by now.

The two men were dressed in typical security contractor garb: sand and OD-colored 511 brand clothing, with sand-colored plate carriers and un-bloused desert boots. No rifles, just sidearms-attached Han Solo-style, as Paul liked to call it, on their thighs.

You got to be fucking kidding me, Paul thought, as he donned his own OD green-plate carrier and locked an OD-green PMAG magazine into his rifle. Paul then worked the charging handle, loading the chamber, and switched the selector switch to FIRE.

The two contractor-types took the sidewalk, then the driveway towards the front door, going around the tall grass of Paul's front yard, as if there had never been a national emergency. Paul heard one of them knocking. Paul put his Peltor headphones on, followed by his own K-pot on top, positioning the four-point chinstrap onto his chin. He slid the screen-less window of his study open and peeked through it with just the right half of his face, his rifle held below the window sill, his trigger finger outside of the trigger guard.

"What do you want?"

"Captain Severn? We're here from the Department of Homeland Security. How are you today?"

"Could be better. Some assholes decided to start a nuclear war. You wouldn't happen to know anything about that, would you?"

"Sir, we were attacked by the Chinese, in an unprovoked attack."

"Really? And who forced them to make that decision?" Paul

knew he was starting to speculate within a vacuum here, as he really didn't know what was going on. But he had his usual inductive hunch, which had always served him well as a military intelligence officer.

"Sir, as you are aware, the country's in trouble. The Chinese hit us hard. Certain parts of the country have been wiped out. Washington DC, San Diego, Los Angeles, and everything from Lewis-McChord, on-north. The President is gone. They didn't hit everything, though. We need your help."

"The President of what?" Paul couldn't resist. He was actually having fun with this.

The two Homeland Security men looked at each other. They didn't seem to get the joke, for a second. The same person continued: "Well anyway, we were sent to this area to recruit anybody in an inactive or retired status who want to be reinstated on active duty at their previous rank. We need your help sir. The country is now officially at war."

"*My country*, or the U.S. Government? You ass-clowns have been pushing the Russians and Chinese militarily for years now. Not real bright, considering what they can hit us with. The U.S. has just been a dying empire with a lot of talk, of late. Remember?"

"Sir, we're just here to offer you the opportunity to serve your country in time of war."

While they continued talking to him, mentioning the President's appeal to all military veterans and retirees, Paul scanned the perimeter for a brief second, to see if anyone had accompanied his visitors.

Emily.

He turned his head slightly to his left. "How are we doing Emily," Paul yelled out.

"Emily!"

"Everything's fine. There's no one back here," she yelled back.

Paul looked back at the two DHS contractors. "I don't give a fuck about your war. Or your President."

"You and your loved ones will have the full protection of the DOD, Homeland Security, and FEMA," the other one of the pair added.

"Wow. And for a minute I thought you guys were really with the IRS," Paul replied dryly. He realized how pissed-off he was now, knowing that he would probably never collect on his Army Reserve retirement, since the US government was not going to survive this anyway. *He and Emily* might not survive this. This was the main reason for his collapse-oriented preps: an alternate retirement plan. "You know something? It used to actually mean something, to be in my former business. But after 9/11, when everybody from the Army on-up had to up their intelligence agencies by 200%, it turned into amateur hour overnight. Even the Soviets never got this stupid with their intelligence structure. I knew you ass-clowns were going to reap what you sowed someday. And I knew that somebody would be begging me to come back to the corporation."

The agent holding the file folder replied. "Sir, you may not be aware of this, but a Continuity of Government operational plan has been instituted, temporarily suspending the Constitution of the United States. If you decide to refuse your reinstatement, your name will stay on the list with about 400,000 other people who are to be apprehended in accordance with this implementation."

"Wow. You guys must really be proud of your jobs," Paul replied sarcastically. From open sources, Paul was familiar with the federal government's Continuity of Government, or COG plan to "temporarily" suspend the U.S. Constitution in the event of a national emergency. Although he had done a little bit of snooping once while on active duty, he had never actually came across anything on this subject. It must have been higher than TOP SECRET, and/or had a really tight "need to know."

Suddenly, Paul started thinking. Access to DHS's resources? His whole reason for being a survivalist was to stay at the top of the societal food chain while every other idiot out there suffered and struggled. Besides, his friends at their emergency retreat would love for him to have this type of access, something he was even asked about in a conversation once, years ago. Hmm... A billion rounds of ammunition, Paul jokingly thought to himself, recalling some stories in the media from years ago. The currency of the 21st century, he used to tell his friends. "Well, I guess I join up one way or another."

"If you come with us, we'll transport you and any loved ones to a safe location where you'll be in-processed and issued uniforms."

"Bullshit," Paul said.

"This is a straight-up offer."

"I'll think about it. Where do I report to?"

"It's... uh, the Portland MEPS center. We can transport you there."

"The MEPS center," Paul asked. The MEPS, or Military Examination and Processing Center was just across the Columbia River, near the Portland Airport.

"Yes sir. Do you have any transportation?"

"I'll figure it out." He wasn't about to blow his OPSEC, especially with these clowns.

"Well, have a good day sir," the DHS agent replied, as he and his partner turned away.

* * *

"Well, I'd say that was a perfect little display of our defenses," Senator Durham said. He was conducting another scheduled administrative meeting with the support staff of Site R.

"The only problem is that in a more normal world, it *would* have been a good display. We just lost two security personnel, one of our perimeter miniguns, and a number of POV's. If anything, we could have used the gasoline in those vehicles to supplement our own supply," the Army Colonel in charge of security said. "In the current environment, with limited resources, we can't afford to take any losses at all."

"Hmm... I see," the senator said. He thought silently for a moment. "How are the rest of our supplies doing?"

"As you know senator, we've grown hugely here at Raven Rock since 9/11. We have months, if not years of supplies for the roughly 1600 personnel that were intended to support COG operations here on the military side, including an indefinite water supply from the artesian spring that flows inside Raven Rock. For food, we've got pallets of freeze-dried food that was manufactured by a contractor just for COG operations. Backing that up we have even more pallets of good old MRE's. During the recent confusion when the alert was given to evacuate to COG locations, only half of the assigned people arrived anyway, so we're pretty well-set."

"I see."

The Army colonel continued, turning some pages in a laminated, loose-leaf binder.

"However, our fuel situation is very different. We generate our own electricity using a pair of diesel generators. Again, we only have enough fuel for six months of operations."

"Do we have any other supply dumps outside of this place," Senator Durham asked.

"Yes sir, we have a number of FEMA supply depots between here, Mount Weather and ABL in West Virginia. Most of them were intended for natural disasters, but we have priority over all of them, needless to say."

"What about the local economy or local resources?"

"As you know, sir, we are authorized under Executive Orders to appropriate whatever we need from the local civilian population," the colonel said.

"Oh great, probably the same people who just attacked us," the senator said.

"That seems to be the case. We didn't find any identification on the bodies, but it's most likely that they're from this area."

* * *

"You're doing what," Emily yelled her question at Paul.

"Yeah, these DHS clowns want me to report to MEPS in Portland. They claim I'll be reappointed as a Captain."

"I thought you weren't going to be involved with the military, again."

"That's right, I wasn't. And in this case, I don't plan on staying long. I was thinking: What if I went ahead and sent you, along with all the preps, to Tim's place? Then I arrive later, but with some goodies, if you know what I mean."

"I don't know. It sounds risky."

"They're desperate. They said I'm on a list of retired reservists, to be reappointed as officers. If I refuse, I'll be placed on a COG round-em-up list to be detained in some FEMA camp or worse. At least that's what they said."

"I don't know... They might come after you."

"With what? And where?"

"I don't know..."

"Look. I'll do my due diligence. You know, recon what's going on out there, stuff like that. Besides, that's just my game," Paul told her. He couldn't resist quoting Doc Holliday from the movie *Tombstone*, for some reason.

"Yeah, you should check this whole thing out before you do anything, instead of having us bug out when we may not need to."

* * *

It was night time, two full days after the two DHS agents had arrived at the house. Paul was riding his 2004 Yamaha TW200 in the breakdown lane of I-5 South, towards the I-205 interchange. He was traveling in a demilitarized ensemble: jeans with an old black ski jacket with purple trim. Instead of his usual mil-spec Danners, Paul wore a short-cut version of the same boot, which would appear more civilian under close scrutiny. In addition to a large pair of protective goggles, Paul rode wearing his PVS-14 night vision monocular with the "J" arm positioning the monocular over his right eye, attached to a black head harness. Over that he wore a coyote-colored fleece hat. Around his nose and face, he wore an OD-green tubular piece of fleece, cinched over his nose and mouth, as a windbreak. On his back, he had a cheap small black backpack, bought years ago: He wanted something civilian-looking for this trip without MOLLE loops all over it. At least it was solid-colored, and not camouflage or OD green.

In a mesh pouch on the side of the backpack was one of his two Nalgene-brand civilian one-quart canteens in coyote color, matching the shape and size of the original military version. It sat inside of a military-issue canteen cup, the only real giveaway of any military-oriented gear.

Paul had also done his own pre-combat check by putting his small backpack on and jumping up and down, seeing what was creating any noise. He would identify the noise, and re-secure, or re-pack that part of his equipment.

The small motorcycle itself was tactically blacked-out: No headlight, brake light, etc. He had entered I-5 South from a person-sized hole in a barbed-wire fence, while also having to negotiate a wide drainage ditch alongside the freeway. Paul had originally found the hole in the barbed-wire one day when running along an old county road, parallel to the southbound side of I-5. Paul originally thought of taking side roads, but figured there would be an even greater chance of running into a prepped neighborhood that would shoot first.

Paul loved this little workhorse of a motorcycle. It could do things that his larger KLR650 couldn't do. He had also installed a short length of T-post to the front of the motorcycle, with a sharpened indentation ground into the front of it. It was an idea he had gotten from Jim Rawles' novel *Patriots*, where members of the group had welded one onto the front of a Ford Bronco for an interstate rescue mission, in the event of any head-severing wire traps.

Abandoned vehicles littered the freeway, particularly in the slow and breakdown lanes. As he rode without headlights or brake lights at about 40 miles per hour, Paul was not seeing any sign of ambush, such as people, or vehicles positioned in any way that would indicate a kill zone. Too lazy to even operate as bad guys, he thought to himself.

Paul pulled off the freeway just before hitting the Glen Jackson Bridge, the huge bridge over the Columbia River connecting the eastern halves of Vancouver, Washington, and Portland, Oregon. Suddenly he got an idea.

He turned the bike around and rode the small motorcycle up the freeway on-ramp overpass for HWY 14 East, then stopped the bike. This gave him a high vantage-point view of the freeway bridge below. Through the night vision monocular still attached to his head, Paul didn't see anyone on the massive bridge's roadway. At least not on this northern half of it. Just a lot of scattered vehicles. His biggest concern was that, with this large man-made choke-point, someone would at least try to control access across the bridge.

Paul turned around, going back down the overpass. He then looked for the entrance to the pedestrian/ bicycle lane and took that across the bridge. It was virtually a road itself through the center of the north and south lanes, but with waist-high cement walls on each side, along with an even higher, square-rectangular designed steel railing. Paul felt fairly safe using this as an avenue of approach.

As he headed south on the freeway's central bicycle path, Paul saw a clump of something in front of him between the concrete sides of the bicycle lane. Surely if it was a person, they would have already been alerted to his motorcycle's engine. Paul slowed the small motorcycle, shifted into neutral and pulled Emily's 9mm Glock from a Blackhawk holster attached to his right side. He held the pistol in his left hand, while passing whatever it was, pointing the pistol at it, Paul suddenly felt like vomiting: The extremely old rotten-meat smell of a dead body overwhelmed him.

Paul stopped the bike in order to heave. Fortunately it didn't come, as he regained his composure. Again, that smell of rotten meat, of corpses.

As Paul rounded a large bend in the middle of the bridge near Government Island, he saw people about a quarter of a mile away. He stopped the bike and killed the engine. They were sitting on the hoods of some vehicles, in the north-bound lane. Three of them. In this new, quiet world, they heard the motorcycle, and looked in his direction. They each got off of their derelict vehicles and began walking in his direction, taking position with rifles over the tops of some vehicles.

Leaning forward to minimize his profile while keeping the front brake locked with his right hand, Paul swung his right leg around the back of the motorcycle in a slowly executed reverse roundhouse kick movement. He would have liked to lay the just-under 200 lb. motorcycle on its side, but the fuel in the tank was precious, at least for this trip, and he didn't want any leaking out of the fuel cap on top of the tank. He went ahead and locked the front wheel, just in case anyone else noticed the motorcycle there..

OK, Paul thought. The good news was that they weren't using any night vision devices. Apart from that, this was going to be a long night. He was going to have to take his time here.

After about 15 minutes, the three men wandered aimlessly, then sat again on the hoods of their vehicles. The TW200 was a relatively quiet motorcycle to begin with. They may have thought it was just another sound in the distance, from the Vancouver side of the Columbia River.

Paul knelt down, continuing to observe them. At the instant that all three of them had their faces turned away from him, Paul instantly and quietly climbed through the left-side of the square-shaped metal railing.

While kneeling down behind a red sedan and trying to keep an eye on them, Paul took off his backpack and pulled a fat, cylindrical-shaped object, painted in flat OD-green out of his backpack. It had originally been an oil filter but now had a threaded flash suppressor inserted inside of it, JB-welded in place, effectively becoming a suppressor. Initially Paul had to use a one-inch hole-cutting drill attachment at the screw-end of the filter to allow for the flash suppressor to go completely inside of it. Paul then drilled a hole at the other end of the filter, creating a straight path for the bullet. He had then used a rat-tail file and sandpaper to widen the exit hole slightly and remove any burrs prior to painting.

Paul spun his homemade suppressor onto the outer threading of his 6-½-inch competition-grade barrel. Paul pulled one of two 17-round magazines, with the word SUBSONIC on a black-on-white printed label, from an electronic printer. It was completely loaded with 147-grain, sub-sonic 9mm rounds. More bullet than powder in the cartridge, which just happened to make the round sub-sonic. He locked the mag, then loaded a round into the chamber of the OD-colored Glock 17 as quietly as he could. He wasn't worried about hiding the sound of his gunshots from these three: He was more worried about anyone else who might be on the bridge, or on the Oregon side of it.

He also pulled a sheathed 4-1/2-inch Ontario RD-4 Bush knife out of his backpack, undoing his leather civilian-style pants belt and slid the sheath onto the right side of it. Hopefully he wouldn't need it. He had the MOLLE sheath for this knife custom-made so that he could draw and strike in one movement, with the knife already held in a proper reverse grip, blade facing down and forward. He loved this knife. It was like love at first sight when he had first bought it. Whenever he did a grip change from reverse to forward grip and back, it literally spun in his hand.

The three individuals still appeared oblivious. In a crouch, Paul began traveling towards them, using the stalled cars as concealment. His Danner boots provided excellent noise discipline. At each stalled vehicle, he would stop and check on the three to make sure that he wasn't detected.

As Paul got closer, he could hear them but not make out any words. They were unintelligible mumblings. Paul's heart was pounding in his ears as he got to within 50 feet of them on the north-bound slow lane.

What if he had a misfire? Could he get all three of them? Their heads were not any larger than the steel target plates that he'd shot at in competitions, over the years.

Suddenly, Paul had an idea. There was garbage laying here-and-there, mostly broken-off auto body parts, shattered automobile glass, children's toys.

Paul headed farther south, going past the three individuals, in order to get behind them. He found a small chunk of shattered safety glass from one of the stalled cars. Holding the suppressed pistol by its frame in his left hand, he picked it up. Remaining crouched, he then started his approach towards them, using the stalled vehicles as cover.

Paul moved towards them at an angle, so that they would all be in a straight line relative to him. He could still hear his own heartbeat. He grabbed the front of the PVS-14 still attached to his head, focusing it for close-up. He also adjusted the electronic gain. His mental focus was like that of a laser beam. As he got within 20 feet of the nearest brigand, he threw the chunk of glass as far as he could towards the direction of his motorcycle, without making noise at his position.

Suddenly, there was a several-part noise from the north.

What's that, one of them asked his friends. They all looked in the direction of the sound, using a single dark-colored sedan for cover.

Paul jumped up from his crouch, sprinting straight at his first target, the pistol facing skyward in his right hand. He brought the pistol down into a good two-handed position, his homemade suppressor almost touching the first man's head.

THWACK ... THWACK ... THWACK! He stopped his sprint several yards after hitting the third guy in the head, point-blank. He turned and with his weapon, scanned the three bodies for movement. There was none.

* * *

Using his night vision monocular, Paul scanned the nighttime area over the top of his OD-green oil filter suppressor. He didn't see anyone else.

As tired as he now was, Paul began the process of checking these guys out. The last one he killed was armed with a Hi-Point 9mm carbine. Paul laughed when he saw it. A Hi-Point. Stupid fucks. He had once rebuilt one of these in a barter deal with one of the two mechanics who helped him restore his 1990 Dodge diesel. When he had test fired the weapon at 25 yards, he was actually impressed by its accuracy and reliability. The downside was the rest of the weapon. They were made for the bargain basement market: cheap plastic toy-like stocks, along with an ungodly recoil due to a huge rectangular-shaped solid steel bolt, actuated with an extremely weak return spring, to ensure reliable cycling. In addition, this carbine used single-stack magazines, limiting its firepower. Paul usually referred to this carbine as a Columbine Special.

The second one Paul off'd had a Chinese SKS with a short barrel. The only difference between this weapon and an AK was that this one was more of a hassle, with its permanently attached magazine. Another bottom-of-the-barrel weapon.

The first one he had killed was armed with an M4, with the typical adjustable stock. It was good that he got this guy first. It was pretty beat-up. It had once been DuraCoated in a mall ninja pink and black tiger-striped pattern. It had probably been jacked from the owner who had done the actual DuraCoat job on it. Or maybe that was several owners ago. How would anyone know? Who really cared?

Paul checked their pockets carefully by pressing each pocket initially, something he once learned from law enforcement, in the event of hypodermic needles, razor blades, or other sharps. Only one of them had any ID on them. The address on the driver's license was Gresham, Oregon. Go figure, Paul thought. He had warned people over the years that Portland's population density, from the West Hills on-east to the other side of Gresham was unreal, somewhere between that of Seattle and San Francisco.

Paul went ahead and stashed the weapons under the rear seat of an old sedan with a ripped-up interior and shattered bits of safety glass all around. Just like you would find in a wrecking yard, back in the day. He grabbed-up all of the extra ammo off their bodies, which wasn't much: Roughly 50-100 rounds for each weapon, all in small, loose piles. He stored the extra 5.56/.223, 9mm, and 7.62x39mm with the weapons. He could check it all out later, but for now he would stick with his own ammo, since his life was currently depending on it. He headed back to the motorcycle inside the cement-walled pedestrian lane.

When Paul got back to the motorcycle, he got a great idea! Why not just coast the bike downhill towards the other end of the bridge? He already had the bike in neutral when he saw the dirtbags. It was virtually all downhill to the Oregon side of the Columbia.

He still couldn't believe that *someone* wasn't controlling the bridge. DHS, some Army National Guard under FEMA, law enforcement, some gang, or rogue former elements of all-of-the-above. Portland really had turned into a human grocery store, just as Paul had warned people, all those years. He felt like he was entering a giant ghetto, on steroids.

Snuffy

* * *

A prudent man foreseeth the evil and hideth himself: But the simple pass on, and are punished.

‒ Proverbs 22:3 (KJV)

As Paul coasted the motorcycle down the center of the Glen Jackson Bridge, he didn't see anyone. He was actually enjoying this. Silent *and* invisible. Paul had never gotten around to painting this bike like the KLR650. Just the front headlight cowling of which he had had black Line-X applied to years ago, while getting the floor of his 1995 Nissan truck done in the same material. The rest of the bike was white, with a metallic gray fuel tank. Since then, he had learned through research just how bad black was as a camouflage color. However, in this instance of driving through the blackest of black nights due to the absence of any urban light pollution, it seemed to work.

As Paul reached Airport Way, he suddenly realized how tired he was. He needed rest, real quick, as his eyes were starting to close. After all, he was an early-50-something playing the shoot-'n-scoot game of a 20-something. He was so tired, he was laughing to himself. For some strange reason, he started thinking of the dialogue during the prison-planet scene from the movie *The Chronicles of Riddick*:

"*I didn't come here to play 'who's the better killer.'*"
"*But it's my favorite game... Haven't you heard?*"

Paul knew an area that he used to use as an off-road shortcut on his larger motorcycle, years earlier. It was a strip of disused road on the east side of the freeway, alongside and below its north-bound side. On the other side of this strip of land was the parking lot for a Home Depot and a 7-11 gas station, lined with trees and boulders, serving as barriers. Needless to say they never worked on a KLR650. He should be able to find something there.

Instead of making a right towards the airport he turned the TW200 west and found a hole in the cyclone fencing there, large enough for him and the small motorcycle. He rode the bike north until he found something that he could hide himself and the bike in, until daylight. There were a couple of trees with some barrier boulders placed near them, next to the side of the old Home Depot. There was also a large shrub of some sort, there. Perfect. Paul still didn't want to lay the small motorcycle on its side. Instead, he pushed it inside of the large shrub.

Paul pulled-out his woodland camouflage military poncho and threw it over the back half of the bike. He then pulled-out of his backpack a MURS-band hand-held transceiver, along with a Dakota Alert motion detector, both set on the same MURS sub-channel. Paul had painted the motion detector in flat brown, since he didn't like the gray, shiny color of the original plastic case. He re-installed the loose AA battery that he had stored inside of the unit, completing the six-battery circuit. It had no on/off switch. Paul walked across this rectangular area of ground to the cyclone fence there, somewhere just under 100 yards from his campsite. He set the sensor on the ground, aiming it directly at his campsite. He then turned-on the MURS hand-unit. With an ear-bud speaker plugged into the two-way radio, he waved his hand in front of the round opening of the Dakota Alert.

A female voice was heard through his earbud: *Alert Zone One...* *Alert Zone One... Alert Zone One.* It worked. It would now detect anything approaching within 100 yards of the motion sensor. Being far enough away, it should also detect anyone walking towards his campsite, from either side. The motion sensor was far enough however, that Paul, laying on the ground on the other side of his motorcycle, inside the shrub, wouldn't set it off.

Paul grabbed another folded-up military poncho; this one in plain OD green, along with a quilted, woodland leaf-patterned poncho liner. He tied the poncho liner's built-in tassels to the grommets on the underside of the poncho, making a by-the-book, improvised, water-resistant sleeping bag. Paul then crawled into the largest opening he could find, inside the large shrub. A lilac shrub? Emily was more expert on these things. With the suppressor removed and loaded with +P+ 9mm, Paul jacked a round in the chamber of the Glock, and put it and the MURS hand-held inside the folded-in-half poncho/poncho liner with him, ear-bud speaker in his right ear.

As Paul worked on falling asleep, he entertained himself by switching frequencies on the MURS hand-held, just to see if anyone was dumb enough to talk on one of the five main channels. He didn't hear anyone transmitting. After going back to Ch. 3, Sub-channel 15, he curled himself up in the poncho inside the shrub, next to his motorcycle and drifted off to sleep.

* * *

Paul awoke to a gray, drizzly dawn. He saw no one around him. Sitting up with his poncho and poncho liner around him, he thought he'd get a cup of coffee going. From his backpack, he pulled-out his alcohol cat stove and an old, small plastic water bottle, with the word ALCOHOL written on it, on a piece of OD duct tape. Paul poured the alcohol into the cat stove, then lit it with a match from a saved matchbook from an MRE. He warmed his hands over the large flame as he waited for it to warm-up. After putting some water in it he then sat the canteen cup directly on top of the burning cat food can. As it heated the water, he gathered-up his stuff, and re-packed it. Paul then walked over and retrieved the Dakota Alert sensor. Paul then finished-off the rest of his two one-quart canteens, since he could refill from the Columbia River, just a short distance away. He also placed the Glock into his horizontal cross-draw holster, under his left armpit. Paul didn't like the idea of carrying anything locked and cocked, but for all intents and purposes he was now in combat.

With the water brought to a boil, he added some instant coffee from a snack-size zip-lock bag, then sat there cross legged, watching the area around him and thinking about last night's events.

Then, his thoughts drifted to those two goons who showed up at his door, two days earlier. He had detected some deceit in their neurolinguistics; their facial cues, as they spoke. A skill he had learned while working counterintelligence, years ago. He still thought this was worth checking out, however...

He pulled the small motorcycle out of the large shrub, started it up, and headed north to the Columbia River, where he rode down the other side of the dike, filled his canteens, and added two water purification tablets to each one. He then rode back towards his campsite, continuing towards Cascade Station.

Cascade Station was another typical big-box retail American

abomination, prior to the attack. What had once been native grassland had been turned into an IKEA, Staples, Best Buy, etc. The MAX-line's light rail station here had once sat in the middle of this grassland field for a number of years, in an idyllic, surrealistic setting with nothing around it, almost like something out the old TV show *Little House on the Prairie*. Obviously, it was only in preparation for the inevitable garbage of modern, big-box consumerist society.

This time however, everything looked different. Everywhere Paul looked there was huge graffiti painted on every single building. The landscaped grass was now over two feet tall. Garbage was strewn everywhere. It reminded Paul of the old John Carpenter film *Escape From New York*.

Oh yeah... Showtime, Paul thought to himself, smiling.

Paul rode his small motorcycle onto the sidewalk, straight towards the huge blue IKEA building, then the parking lot next to it. He traveled behind all of the other big-box stores, in the direction of the airport.

He headed west towards the Target store there, with its own separate parking lot. Wait a second, Paul thought. An FBI building was on the other side of the MAX line, next to the Target. Paul decided to turn around, and go southeast, and circle the business park, where the Portland MEPS was located.

As he drove through some parking lots Paul found a commercial building on NE Alderwood Road. He pulled into its parking lot, which was about 300 yards from the front of the MEPS entrance, with some old cropland, in-between. Perfect, Paul thought. From here, he could conceal the motorcycle, and observe the front of the MEPS center. From here, Paul pulled-out a Vortex-brand monocular, and started observing.

For roughly half an hour, Paul didn't see anything.

Then, Paul noticed a school bus-sized bus pull up in front of the

MEPS building. It was white-colored with the US Homeland Security logo printed on the side. When it stopped, there was no activity for about five minutes.

Then, he saw a line of men, all shackled together, dressed in everyday-civilian clothing, all heading into the MEPS building.

What the hell, Paul thought. This used to be a MEPS center, a place where young men and women were tested and examined, while looking forward to careers in the US military. Now it was disgraced, being used for what was left of the police state.

As they finished shuffling into the building, guided by some men in black uniforms, Paul thought he'd better check this out from another angle. He started up the bike, this time heading north on 82nd Avenue, towards the Portland Airport.

While on 82nd near the Marriott Hotel, Paul turned left and went through a vehicle-sized hole in the fence that surrounded the airport's runway. He headed towards a pair of trees on the inside of that fence. The fence had those brown plastic strips in it, to conceal any view. This would be another angle to view MEPS from. He steered the motorcycle back towards the fence, shifting into neutral, then killing the ignition, coasting to a stop.

However, from here, all he could see was the side of the single-story MEPS building.

Suddenly, a white Ford Explorer in the same Homeland Security logo entered the same hole in the fence that Paul had just driven through, heading towards him.

He was screwed.

* * *

The path of the righteous man is beset on all sides by the inequities of the selfish, and the tyranny of evil men...

– Ezekiel 25:17

OK, Paul thought. Plan B. He simply stood there, waiting for them. Stay focused, he thought to himself. You're probably not going to survive this, anyway.

The white Ford Explorer stopped about 20 feet in front of Paul. Two men, dressed in black uniforms with matching plate carriers and M4 rifles on three-point slings in front of them stepped-out of the vehicle, and approached him.

"What are you doing here?"

"Me? I was just driving by, trying to find some food for my family," Paul said, in a nerdy voice, gesturing with his hands in front of him. This impersonation was usually pretty convincing, as people used to tell Paul that he looked like the kind of person who "wasn't into firearms." Paul had briefed his loved ones years ago that when cornered, and he starts his innocent nerd impersonation, to get ready to either run, or fight.

"There's supposed to be another MRE distribution next week, here in Portland. You're not supposed to be around here."

"Where did you get the fuel for the bike," the other uniformed officer asked.

Paul had a feeling that these must be FEMA contractors. Pass some basic certifications and no matter what an uneducated or unskilled dirt-bag you were, you got to be a hired gun. He had seen this with the aftermath of Hurricane Sandy, years ago.

"I've just had it in the tank of this bike for a long time. I haven't ridden it lately," Paul said, in his innocent, nerdy, frightened voice. It wasn't actually too far from the truth. On both counts.

"Well, we're going to need to confiscate the motorcycle, as per FEMA Directives."

"Uh,...OK, it's yours, take it. Uh,...I don't want any trouble," Paul said, as he stepped farther away from the bike, same nerdy, yuppie voice, hands gesturing upward, palms facing them. The officer who asked about the motorcycle then walked over to it, and began fiddling with it.

"What's in the backpack," the other officer asked.

"Uh...nothing. Here, take a look," Paul said as he took the backpack off and handed it to the officer with his left hand, right hand kept in the air. Paul could feel his heart beating, again. This is it. Paul almost thought he was seeing his life play-out in front of him.

As Paul handed him the backpack, in one quick movement, he grabbed the DHS officer's right hand with his left, twisting the officer's hand against his wrist, pressing his thumb into the metacarpal area in the back of the DHS guy's hand. As the DHS guy instinctively pulled his hand back in pain, Paul still holding on with his left, Paul drew the Glock 17 under his left armpit in his jacket, with his right. The black-uniformed guy started going to his knees. BAM! A round into the DHS guy's left eyeball. As the officer fell, Paul fell with him, spinning, keeping the wounded officer between him and the other live one.

The other DHS goon pointed his M4 rifle at Paul and fired, filling the back of his buddy's plate carrier with a three-round burst of 5.56mm. Laying on the ground with the other black-uniformed goon on top of him, Paul fired single-handed at the other DHS man. BAM! BAM! BAM! BAM! BAM! BAM! BAM! Paul walked the rounds up the DHS man's chest, into his face, focusing on the pistol's front sight, the DHS man himself a blur. The officer put his hands to his face and screamed, falling backwards.

I got to get this guy off me! There could be more of them, Paul thought to himself. The guy on top of Paul was kind of fat and out of shape, to begin with. Paul rolled him off of him. These stupid fucks. Fatherland security. I've got something for you neo-nazi motherfuckers, Paul thought to himself. He was on the warpath.

Paul ran to the second one he had shot, landing a knee on his chest, pinning the rifle there, still attached to its three-point sling.

"You're 'gonna take *my* bike, motherfucker," Paul shot his question at him. Paul hit him in the face with the Glock. A round looked like it had hit the DHS man's cheekbone, shattering it as it glanced-off, along with a hole in his neck, spurting blood.

"Don't kill me," the black uniform said, quietly

"I can't believe you've been alive this long, you stupid little fuck. 'The fuck's going on around here?"

"DHS Internment Processing Facility," the dying DHS goon said, straining on every word.

"Who are they picking up?"

"People on a list..."

"What list?"

"Before the war," the DHS man said quietly.

"Anything military going on here?"

"No..."

"Motherfuckers..."

Paul stood up, grabbing the man's rifle, pulling it off from around the mortally wounded man's body. He also pulled the DHS man's tactical vest off of him. He went over to the other one he had shot in the eye and grabbed-up the other DHS man's M4, and TAC vest. Picking up his small black backpack, Paul then spun his oil filter suppressor back onto the front of his Glock, dropping the magazine, ejecting a live +P+ round into the air, catching it in his left hand, then loading his second mag of subsonic 9mm. He then went over to their vehicle. He fired one round into each tire, then looked for the fuel tank. Then, standing next to a wheel as cover, he reached under the vehicle, putting a round in the fuel tank. Paul knew it wasn't like the movies, where putting a round in the fuel tank would blow it up. Even with tracers or incendiary ammunition, it was hard to do, with a single round. He did hope that the round did more than one hole's worth of damage, however. He looked underneath, to make sure it was draining.

"Bye assholes," Paul said aloud. With the fuel leaking, Paul then fired a glancing round at the fuel tank where the fuel was leaking, making a spark which, with the proper fuel/air mixture started it burning. With his backpack, both M4's slung cross-shoulder on his back, and sitting on both TAC vests draped over his seat, Paul leaned over the handlebars as he hauled-ass out of there, heading south on 82nd Avenue.

Paul continued south on 82nd to Columbia Boulevard, underneath it, circling around, and taking it east. He didn't see anyone following him.

As Paul approached the Holiday Inn on Columbia, a pickup truck with an M2 .50 cal. Browning Machinegun on a tripod suddenly blocked his path. In an open field to his right a motorcycle appeared with two people on it, wearing full-face helmets. They skidded to a stop, just a few yards away to his right. Paul was now trapped in a crossfire, if anyone decided to throw lead.

Paul skidded to a stop. He saw what looked like a hopeless situation, for the moment. He went ahead and put his hands up. It didn't mean he wasn't going to go without a fight.

"YA YA YA YA YA" someone yelled from the motorcycle. Then a raspberry sound, like a little kid would make, while sticking their tongue out. "Who are you motherfucker!"

* * *

Paul pulled his coyote-colored fleece hat off, keeping his hands in the air. After his heart had already skipped a few beats, Paul suddenly relaxed, then just looked straight ahead at the technical truck with the .50 cal., in disbelief. "I know that voice" he said aloud, shaking his head slightly. "My name's Paul."

"Paul, right?" The other motorcyclist pulled his white with black designs helmet off. "It's me, Ronald, you motherfucker! WASSAP!"

Paul turned his head towards him, smiling, and shaking his head.
"Motherfucker... Nothing. Just trying to survive a nuclear war. What the fuck are *you* doing," Paul asked, smilingly.
"YO YO YO, stand-down," Ronald yelled at the people in the truck, waving his arms. Ronald got off of his motorcycle and walked towards Paul, as Paul threw his kickstand down, and got off of his. Ronald's was a 250 cc Honda dirt bike. They walked towards each other, smiling. "Wassap," Ronald yelled again.
"How's it going," Paul asked. They gave each other a hug. Ronald was in his forties, with dark, short-shaven hair, with gray in it. He was about Paul's height, just under six-feet.
"What the fuck are you doing around here?" Raspberry sound. "This is a bad fucking place."
"You know, for some reason I always knew I'd run into you, post-collapse."

Paul had known Ronald from some gun shows that Paul had vended at, years earlier. A goofball with Tourette's Syndrome. However, Ronald had been a good customer, while acquiring massive amounts of firepower at the shows with money he had made from his landscaping business. Everything from .50 BMG ammunition, on-down. All the body armor and ammunition that was either armor piercing, tracer, and/or incendiary, that he could afford. Paul remembered how Ronald used to bring a four-wheeled garden cart with him to the gun shows, the entire thing subdued in flat OD green spray paint.

"Just trying to get some intel. I was told some line about being reappointed as an officer."

"Ya ya ya. Who, those FEMA fucks? They've been rounding people up!"

Paul looked at the guy standing in the back of the truck with the tripod-mounted Ma Deuce. He was dressed in black tactical gear, with a sand-colored Arab-style shemagh, wrapped completely around his head. He was looking at the direction Paul had come from, scanning some billowing smoke in the distance with a pair of binoculars.

"Looks like your buddy did some damage down there," the guy on the .50 said.

Suddenly, there were was another white Ford Explorer police cruiser in the distance, north of them, with flashing lights, heading in their direction, south on 82nd.

The raspberry sound, again. "We need to get the fuck out of here. Let's go to my place."

"Sounds good to me."

* * *

They headed east across I-205 on Columbia Boulevard, then on Sandy Boulevard, in a three-vehicle convoy: Ronald's motorcycle on point, the technical truck about 50 yards behind it, followed by Paul, an equal distance away from the truck, providing some rear security. Not bad, since no planning had been made, prior to their movement, Paul thought. Paul tried his best to be a tail-end Charlie, in order to cover their rear. He looked over his shoulders as much as he could, while also keeping an eye on his rear-view mirrors, for anyone following.

People were on the sidewalks of Sandy Boulevard, many on bicycles. Many of them were in rags, some appearing to wander aimlessly. There was commerce here. Some storefronts with handmade signs advertising clothing, cigarettes, liquor, marijuana. They couldn't have been the previous property owners, Paul thought. The small-timers in this new economic order were relegated to lean-to's on the sidewalks, made out of blue tarps, heavy-duty plastic, etc. The merchandise was mostly used shoes, children's clothing, etc. The kind of junk you used to see at low-end flea markets, before the collapse. Some of the people along the sidewalks looked-up in order to take notice of the heavily armed three-vehicle convoy, which was quickly moving east. Apparently, heavily armed groups traveling-by on vehicles no longer drew much attention, other than the occasional look of envy at the new symbols of wealth: Vehicles *and* weapons.

After what seemed like half an hour of fast driving they finally got to Ronald's place near Troutdale, Oregon. It was an old, whitewashed farmhouse on some of the last remaining land in this area which hadn't been developed before the collapse. Everyone came to a stop. Ronald pulled-out what looked like a Baofeng transceiver, speaking into it. Paul continued scanning their rear. Damn, using a radio to re-enter his perimeter, Paul thought. Looks like these people have their game-on.

They parked their vehicles in some gravel, off to the side of the house and headed for the front door.

"Where did you get that Ma-Deuce," Paul asked, thumbing back towards the truck. The machinegun's tripod even had its traverse-and-elevation gear connected between the gun and the tripod, making for extremely accurate long-range fire.

"Yeah. Ya ya ya. I traded a bunch of shit for it from some Oregon Army Guard guys. They didn't have any ammo for it and I did."

"Go figure," Paul said, laughing.

As they entered the house, Paul saw three other people in the living room, who looked like members of some punk rock band.

"YA YA YA! You guys! This is my old buddy Paul! Remember, the guy I told you had all that cool shit for sale, the AP ammo, the razor wire, and all that other shit?"

"Oh, yeah," a youngish-looking guy sitting on a couch said, sporting a pink-colored Mohawk, the sides of his head shaved bald.

"How's it going," Paul asked

"Pretty good," one of them replied.

"Yeah man, come on in," Ronald said. He then bent forward, clenching his fists in front of him. "WOOOHOOO" he yelled, followed by a loud raspberry sound, spittle going everywhere, in an uncontrollable fit.

Paul simply stood there laughing, shaking his head. "You fucking goofball," a term of endearment only two type-A men could understand. "I always knew we'd bump into each other on the other side of collapse. It looks like you ran out of your medications."

"Ya ya ya. Hey, remember? We're living the dream," Ronald yelled, with his hands high in the air.

Years earlier, when Paul had once invited Ronald to sit with him at his gun show table, they had joked about bartering and haggling, as if collapse had already occurred. Paul was now laughing uncontrollably at Ronald, and at the irony of it all. Paul actually liked keeping people around him who made him laugh, and Ronald, a somewhat functional and intelligent adult, used humor to deal with his condition, as many with Tourette's Syndrome had done. He did remember trying to keep Ronald at a certain arms-length, however. When he had his fits, it would be like Moses parting the waves, as far as people were concerned. At least Ronald had been smart enough to live as a survivalist, in preparation for all of this.

Paul was still laughing. "Yeah, a post-collapse nightmare. Our dream."

Ronald laughed a nervous little laugh, like some little kid commenting on another kid caught with his hand in the cookie jar. "Hoo hoo hoo, man, taking-on those DHS assholes. You're a lucky motherfucker,"

"How's that?"

"They always keep an MRAP and a Bradley there at the old MEPS, with belt-feds on top. Ya ya. At least the Bradley. I didn't see either of 'em when we were checking 'em out, this morning. Raspberry sound. Then we saw you, doing your shit down there. Yeah, other than that, they're a joke. They're spread pretty thin. Ya ya ya."

"Well I guess they're even thinner now."

Raspberry sound. "Ya ya ya." He looked at his friends. "See! I told you this guy was a bad motherfucker!"

Paul laughed.

"Hey, what did you get off those guys," Ronald asked. The two government-issue M4's were still slung across Paul's back.

"Yeah, lets, take a look," Paul went ahead and unslung them. They were fairly beat-up looking, possibly old military-issue, from the Iraq War. "Nice. ACOG red dot sights. Looks like government issue. Fully selective, three-round burst."

Next, Paul and Ronald took a look at the vests. Typical mil-spec plate carrier vests, in black. Each one had a radio on its left shoulder, along with ammo pouches full of loaded magazines for the M4's and for the 9mm Beretta M2 pistols each man had worn on their right thighs. Damn, Paul thought. I forgot to get those. He didn't really need any more pistols, anyway. They would have made great barter items, though.

"Yeah" Ronald yelled, followed by another raspberry sound. "Hey man, we should celebrate! Pull-out that bottle of 'Jack and that weed we traded for, last month," Ronald yelled to his friends.

"I don't know, Ronald. I'm pretty tired, already, and I have to keep my edge.".

"Aw, come on man, we haven't seen each other in years. Besides, you're 'gonna have to wait until night-time to get out of here, anyway. We can all party, and you can crash here!"

"Cool, thanks."

* * *

The rest of the day was spent taking hits from a prized bottle of Jack Daniel's, taking a tour of Ronald's cyclone-fenced perimeter, his arsenal inside the house, his large food-producing garden, and taking an occasional puff from a weed-filled pipe. Paul and Ronald were laughing their asses off. And none of this was in any particular order. More out of courtesy than desire, Paul took a small sample of each. Being in good shape as you got older meant a much lower tolerance for alcohol, and since weed had become legal in both Oregon and Washington State years earlier, it hardly drew any fascination for him.

"Oh man, I'm having a great time" Paul said, slapping Ronald on the back.

Ronald returned the gesture. "Yeah man!" Raspberry sound. "It's good to see you again. Hey! You know, you should come down here. Bring your preps and everything down here from Ridgefield. This can be your bug-out retreat."

Oh my God, Paul thought.

"I don't know...Thanks anyway. I really appreciate it, though. Me and the wife are pretty well set. I've had my security up for a long time now, and no one has penetrated it. No real trouble in our area. I think half of my neighbors have already off'd themselves, anyway."

"Yeah, but it's just the two of you."

"That's OK. I've got some force multipliers."

"Yeah." Raspberry sound. "Just like me."

"Pretty much. If we need to, though, it's a deal. I had plans with a buddy of mine, an old timer named Tim with a place outside Molalla. You probably know him, the fat old guy from the gun shows who always wore that black beret? He's an old-school 1970's survivalist. He put together a really large live-in retreat, years before all this. I even have some stuff pre-positioned with him. Not much, just a big tote. The original plan was for me or Emily to get to his place as a safe house, if we got stuck on this side of the Columbia, in a sudden event."

"Yeah, you see, man? That's way down south. You don't want

to travel around Portland, man! It's bad!" Raspberry sound. "There's fucking dead bodies everywhere and groups of these fucking punks setting-up ambushes everywhere on the freeways. That's why we haven't had to worry about much out here. They're all smoking each other."

"Yeah... I'd be cutting in this direction anyway, *then* heading south," Paul said. He *could* use Ronald's place as an *en route* safe house in that event, but nothing more. Regardless, Paul did not want to bug out south of the Columbia River. And, hunkering down with Ronald and his people was completely out of the question.

"I need to get some rest, and then head out of here tonight, if that's OK with you."

"Yeah, sure man. Ya ya ya."

Paul had been formulating something else, at least subconsciously, while they had been talking. "By the way, since they might be looking for me tonight, maybe you could help me out, and set-up a diversion, so I can get back across the bridge."

"Like what?"

"Like maybe fire a couple of API rounds into the MEPS center, just in case they're watching the Glen Jackson."

"YA YA YA - are you fucking crazy?"

"They're spread thin, now. You said so, yourself. Just crank that Ma Deuce once to put it into semi-auto mode, and put a couple of rounds into the MEPS, from a thousand yards, out. That wouldn't be too hard, would it? My gut feeling is that they're on their way out, anyway."

"Ya ya. I don't know..."

"How about this: You help me out, and I leave you one of those M4's I got off of those DHS fucks. It's a generous offer," Paul said to Ronald. He wasn't about to lo-ball an old friend, after all.

"Ya ya ya. Oh fuck," Ronald said, as he looked off into the distance over his property. He then looked back at Paul. Raspberry sound. "It's a deal" he said, as he stuck-out his hand to seal it.

Ronald put Paul up that evening in a cluttered room, filled with loose rifle cartridges, various AR and AK magazines and half-open cases of MRE's. The old red shag carpet hadn't been vacuumed in months, if not years. There was barely enough room on the floor for the old Army-issue polypad that Ronald gave him to rest on.

As trashed as the room was, as Paul drifted off to sleep, he was reminded once again. I'm surrounded by a room full of wealth. It was like an image from an old movie, of a cave full of jewelry, gold coins and other riches. People would kill for what was in this room. And this was just *some* of Ronald's larder. Paul was just as well set, if not a little more organized. He had no problem falling asleep.

* * *

Paul awoke. He hit the indiglo backlight on the old cheapo five-dollar watch he used for this trip. 10:37 PM. Using the green LED light on his keychain Paul got up and checked his gear, making sure it was all there. There was some dim light out in the hallway that the room was off-of.

Paul walked out into the living room, filled with dim, white fluorescent lighting. "Hi you guys," he told the group.

Raspberry sound. "Yeah man, we were wondering when you were getting up," Ronald said.
"Well, I'm just about ready to get going. By the way, can I get some coffee, by any chance?"
"Here you go, man." Ronald walked into the kitchen and flung a small packet of Taster's Choice Instant from an MRE towards Paul, like a shuriken throwing star. "Whaa."

Paul caught it with both hands, laughing. "Right on. Thanks."
"Ya ya ya. We got some hot water on top of the wood stove, over there." Ronald pointed to the wood stove with the flat top, in the opposite corner of the wood-paneled room. It had a small stove-top kettle sitting on it.
"Cool, thanks." Paul grabbed his own military-issue canteen cup, and poured the hot water from the small pan into the cup, with the MRE coffee following it. "Yummy."

About 45 minutes later that evening, Ronald and the other people that Paul had encountered the previous day put their same convoy together, but this time with Paul's motorcycle at the front of it. This time, Paul had one of the captured M4's slung on its three-point sling, resting in front of him, facing to the right. This way, he could still control the brakes and the throttle, while firing suppressive rounds with the rifle. They drove a different route back towards I-205, this time taking Halsey Street, then heading north on 82nd Avenue. Then to an unused plot of land, off of Alderwood Road, near where Paul had first spied on the MEPS Center.

Once they arrived there, the line-of-sight distance to the MEPS looked like about 700 yards. Paul helped setup their position, guiding the truck as it backed-up towards the trees, for the M2 to fire through. Paul checked to make sure the .50 BMG cartridges were either blue, or silver-tipped: Armor piercing or armor piercing Incendiary. The first two rounds needed to at least be regular tracer, in order to walk the rounds to the target.

Paul wanted to stay with them to make sure that this part of the plan went OK, before circling back to I-205, then heading north. He was wearing his PVS-14, focused on the distant target. Everyone started putting on hearing protection. Paul inserted the earplugs from around his neck, then donned a borrowed pair of headphones for extra hearing protection. The MEPS building was kept blacked-out, although Paul could just barely make out a faint amount of residual light, coming from under the doors of the main entrance. Ronald was using a cheaper, Russian-made hand-held night vision monocular. Under blackout conditions, they all left their engines running.

"Ya ya ya. Yo Mike, go ahead," Ronald said.

Mike reached over-hand, and yanked-back on the cocking handle. "Here it goes."

BOOM! The first round left a red streak of light, hitting the parking lot in front of the MEPS, ricocheting up into the night sky, to the east.
"A little low," Paul yelled out.
"Got it," Mike said.

BOOM! Another red streak of light, this one going right through one of the MEPS building's front windows.
"YEAH," Ronald yelled in a deep, macho yell.
"Nice! Alright. I'm 'outta here," Paul yelled to Ronald. "Thanks again for everything. Give 'em two more rounds, after I leave, then get the fuck 'outta here." Paul pulled his borrowed headphones off, handing them back to Ronald. They both warmly and quickly shook hands, giving each other a short hug. Nothing

brought men together like being in combat. "Thanks again! Have fun with that M4," Paul yelled to him.

"YA YA YA. Yeah. I'm gonna rebuild the fucker, and put a different upper on it." Paul gave a thumbs-up as he got on the TW200, and sped off to the south, in the direction they had come from. He saw a spotlight come on at the MEPS, looking for where the rounds came from. He heard two more rounds come from the M2, then some small arms fire coming from the direction of the MEPS building. Ronald was keeping his end of the deal. He hoped he and his crew were going to be OK. Ronald might have been a goofball, but he had a good heart.

Although, he had to admit the obvious question to himself: What exactly *was* Ronald doing out there, early that morning, when they encountered each other?

With his newly acquired rifle in front of him, Paul headed north on 205, picking up the bicycle path at Sandy Blvd., safely getting as much speed out of the small motorcycle as he could. He saw a couple of groups of people on the bike path, looking in the direction of the Portland MEPS. Paul watched them closely, as he sped past. They only seemed to notice him once he got close, then they seemed shocked as he sped past them, with no headlight.

* * *

As Paul continued north on the Glen Jackson inside of the enclosed bike path, he was trying to remember where he took-out those three brigands. Finally, he saw it. As Paul approached, he also noticed some refugees on foot, heading north, about 100 yards south of where he had dispatched those three. Shit. It looked like a man, one woman, and two small kids, all wearing backpacks. Should I wait for them to pass? Screw it. I just want to get home, Paul thought. They don't appear to be any threat. He didn't see any weapons on them, through the night vision monocular.

Paul stopped the motorcycle, killing the engine near where he had stashed those weapons. He hopped-over the brown, chest-high rectangular railing, walking towards the wrecked vehicle, while keeping an eye on the refugees, the M4 at the ready, still left-handed.

As he headed back to the bike with an armload of weapons and ammo, the male of the group, long dark hair under a ball cap, approached him.

"Hey man... whoa," he said, as he noticed Paul's PVS-14 monocular and the cross-slung M4, the armload of rifles, then the dead bodies. Mentally, the man suddenly flashed back to a scene from one of the older *Star Trek* movies, involving the Borg. He was scared. "Just wondering if you have any food."

"No, not me. Sorry."

"My wife and kids haven't eaten in two days. We had to get out of Portland...Hey, those weapons... Can you spare one of those? We don't have any."

"Sorry." Paul wasn't about to donate to charity. As sad as it was, these people looked like they were dead people walking, anyway. He couldn't believe these people had survived in Portland, this long. Paul climbed back over the railing, keeping an eye on the guy. He then started securing the rifles to the small cargo rack on the TW200, with a black bunji-net. The man simply stood there.

Paul simply looked back at the guy, still standing there looking at him, with the rest of his family in the background. Paul kept his left hand on the pistol grip of the M4. It looked like Paul needed to maintain his aura, here.

The man finally turned around, heading back towards his family, continuing their trek north.

Paul continued watching him. Suddenly, Paul felt sorry for them. He didn't like always having to use the hardball routine with people, but it was simple procedure if one wanted to stay alive. In this environment any seemingly harmless clown could instantly whip-out a pistol and pop someone. Damn, those kids, he thought. How could he walk away from a couple of kids in need, even if their father's story was BS? Besides, did he really need to waste the space inside his house with this piece-of-shit Hi-Point carbine?

"Hey buddy," Paul yelled to the guy. The family turned around. I'll leave you this nine em-em carbine, and a couple MRE's. Make sure your kids get them. I'll be watching to make sure." He dropped the magazine from the Hi-Point, then worked the carbine's chamber with his right hand, catching the chambered round in the same hand as it tumbled in the air.

"Hey, thanks man. Thanks a lot," the father of the family said, as he walked towards Paul.

"Stop. Stay where you are. I'll take off, and leave the ammo and mag about 100 yards up the bicycle path. You can pick them up there."

"Hey, thanks man."

"No Problem."

Paul set the unloaded carbine and the MRE's on top of the Jersey barrier-type cement, under the brown rectangular metal railing, then got back on the TW 200, and took off quickly. Paul then stopped the motorcycle where he said he would, leaving the magazine and loose 9mm rounds in the middle of the pedestrian lane, as he had promised. Refocusing the PVS-14, he saw the guy struggling to open an MRE, then squatting down, handing the contents to his kids.

As Paul continued north on I-205 through Vancouver, riding tactically in the dirt and grass of the northbound breakdown lane, he began reflecting on all the events that had occurred during this trip. While watching the overpasses, and any other hints of an ambush, he began thinking about the risks of this trip. Emily. My God! What if anything had happened to him, while on this trip? He had made no contingency plan for her. What the hell was he thinking, making this trip? He and Emily were all each other had, except for her relatives, who lived in the area, but had not been heard from. It was just them, and Paul's various force multipliers that kept them safe up to this point: Trip-wired explosive traps, various types of protective wire, night vision, cameras, etc.

He remembered the deceit that he had noticed from the DHS guys. Why did he even make this trip? Paul had watched their eyes as they spoke, which literally worked like the paper passing through a polygraph. At least he had accomplished something: He had made contact with someone he knew, and gained a lot of usable intell at the same time.

The only reason Emily let me go on this trip was because she knows that I always come back, he thought to himself. Time to concentrate on the road.

As Paul was about two miles away from the house at around midnight, he pulled off of the country road, and killed the engine. It was dark out here, due to overcast night skies, and now rain. Not even distant light pollution, anymore. It was almost hard to get used to. Paul decided to take the chance, and pull a small IR flashlight out of his small backpack. To the naked eye, no one saw any visible light come from this device, when turned on. Through a light-amplification night vision device, or digital camera, however, it looked like a flashlight being turned-on.

Between the PVS-14 monocular still attached to his head and the IR flashlight, Paul scanned the area around him. Just some trees here-and-there and some old farmland, on his right-side of the road. To his right, about 300 yards away, down an old gravel road, was an old, dark 1970's-looking single-wide mobile home, which appeared long deserted. It had obviously been grandfathered on that piece of private property. He removed his earplugs in order to perform a listening halt, as well. Paul didn't hear anything in the darkness. He then pulled-out his MURS transceiver to inform Emily that he was about to arrive. He keyed the transmitter. "Emily, This is Paul. Come in, Emily," he said into the MURS transceiver.

"Hold it right there now," an old man's voice suddenly said in the darkness.

Paul spun his head to the right and saw an old gray-haired and gray-bearded man with an AK raised to his shoulder, aimed at him.

* * *

"You got to be fucking kidding me. Not again" Paul said, looking straight ahead, as he lifted both hands into the air, still sitting on the motorcycle.

"What do you mean not again?"

"Buddy, you have no idea what I've already been through, the last two evenings."

"Where did you get all that gear on the back of your motorbike, there?"

"I had to kill a few people."

"You had to kill a few people? Well... I've seen you ride your motorcycle around here before. You live around here, don't you?"

"Yeah, in the neighborhood up ahead."

"Well, you look like you know what you're doing. My name's Bill," he said, as he lowered the Kalashnikov, and extended his right hand to Paul. Paul took it, giving him his usual hard handshake.

"You look like you knew this was coming too, "Bill said.

Paul laughed. "That makes two of us. I can't believe you got the drop on me."

"Well, I saw you through this." The old man showed him what looked like a small, first generation, one-hundred dollar night vision monocular, similar to the one Ronald had.

"Well, that would do it" Paul said, smiling. He didn't even realize that anyone was still living in the old single-wide mobile home. Paul just thought it was an old, derelict trailer, left on some farmer's land.

"How about this. Let me check-in with the wife, then we can talk."

"OK."

Paul then keyed the MURS hand-held, using the MURS sub-channel it was set-to, the same one he had used for the Dakota Alert. "Hello, Emily, this is Paul. I'm coming in." He un-keyed the mike, and waited for her reply.

"Hello Emily" he repeated into the radio, then waited again.

After a moment he got a clear response from her as she operated the base station-setup at the house. "Hi, I'm here. I just woke-up. Thank goodness you're back. I was really worried."

"I know, sweetie. Never again. Stay inside the house. OK?"

"OK."

"Also, I'm going to be a few minutes. I just met one of our neighbors. He lives in that old mobile home we always used to drive past. Condition red. I repeat: Condition red, OK?"

"OK."

"OK, Sweetie. Out here."

"Condition red?"

"Relax. It's just a code. It means things are OK."

"I know it's late, but why don't you come on-in for a drink. I think it's been decades since I've ever had a guest here."

"Sure." Paul didn't read any deception, or get any clues that this was some sort of a trap. Besides, the guy had seen that Paul himself was heavily armed, with his stuff at the ready. He was tired, and just wanted to get home, but at the moment, forming *some* kind of community relations, especially at this stage in the game, was important.

"You can just turn around, and just park in front of the house."

"Actually, I better park behind it."

"Yeah, that sounds good."

After parking the motorcycle in some tall weeds that surrounded the 14 foot-wide trailer and locking his motorcycle's front wheel as a precaution, Paul walked around the old single-wide trailer, still wearing his night vision monocular. He still didn't notice anything suspicious. He made sure that he was inside the trailer with the door closed, so that Bill could turn on some lighting. Bill turned on a small flashlight, shining it on what was actually a nice solid wood table. At least it had been at one time. He then lit an old-fashioned kerosene lamp. It was amazing how it lit-up the entire interior of the heavily cluttered mobile home.

"Have a seat" Bill said, gesturing him towards the table.

Once seated, Paul noticed the cardboard covered windows, along with an old musty smell, the kind of smell that came with an old mobile home that hadn't been gone-over with a bleach solution for a while.

"You like whiskey," Bill asked.

"Yeah sure, thanks."

Bill reached into a cupboard above the gas stove in the kitchen and pulled-out an old bottle of *Maker's Mark* bourbon. Paul actually liked this. Two men talking over a couple of shots of whiskey, in the light of a kerosene lamp. Paul had a feeling there would be some similar interests discussed. This guy was obviously a fellow survivalist. It was the kind of "back to the future" stuff that Paul and some of his collapse theorist friends used to discuss: That the post collapse world would appear more like the days of The Old West, than anything else, *if* we were lucky.

Paul took his small, half-filled glass from Bill.

"Why thank you" Paul said, playing the part. He felt as if he were in 1880's Tombstone.

"Yeah, I've seen you ride around here. From the looks of your motorbike, I'd say you knew what you were doing. Were you in the military?"

"Retired Army intelligence officer."

"Mm hum. Yup, this is my place. I have a garden out back. I've always done canning and dehydrating. I make my own fuel too, but I can't find anymore fry oil. I *was* able to find some used automatic transmission fluid at a couple of repair shops, though, before all this happened."

"You have an older diesel too?"

"Yup, two of 'em. My old Dodge isn't running right now, but my '85 Nissan diesel is."

"You've got an old '80's Nissan diesel? Nice," Paul said approvingly, while sipping from his glass.

"You got a lot of rifles there," Bill said, gesturing back towards the TW200, behind the mobile home.

"Yeah, I got into a little action in Portland. Some five-five-six and some nine millimeter. My main battle rifle back at the house is an M4 chambered in five-four-five Russian, though."

"Oh yeah," Bill said, stroking his beard, just like an old prospector. "The Poison Bullet. That's what they called it in the old Afghan war."

"Mm-hum," Paul said. At that moment, a large, fat long-haired cat, black with some white in its fur struggled to jump into Bill's lap.

Paul laughed. "What's his name?"

"Her. Miss Texaco. That's her name."

"How's she doing? Are you able to keep her fed?"

"Yeah. I take my .22 out to go hunt stuff for her, dress it and cook it for her. Squirrels, chipmunks."

"We still have dry cat food, and some dry dog food. We put-up a good amount of Meow-Mix in mylar bags before all this happened, if you need any. You know how some cats prefer dog food, and visa-verse."

"Yup," Bill said, laughing.

"Well, we can spare the dog food at least, if you need any."

They continued talking for roughly the next 20 minutes, about their gardens, and then back to their diesel trucks. Finally, Paul broke the conversation, standing up out of his chair.

Well, I need to get going. I'm dead tired, and the wife is waiting for me. Are you going to be OK? Anything you need? There might be some bad people, government, or otherwise, coming around here.

Not really. Thanks anyway, though. Miss Texaco could use some of that nice cat food of yours, though. We'll be OK. I've got this AK and a good, scoped Mosin-Nagant, too.

Paul laughed. "Yeah, that old fifty-four-r round will knock someone into next Tuesday." With that, they shook hands, then Paul gathered-up his stuff. "Well, it's been a pleasure. I'll come back to visit when I'm not about to pass-out."

"Yup, anytime. Me and Miss Texaco will be here."

After wading back through the tall weeds and blackberry, Paul re-secured his gear back on the small motorcycle and made his own path going forward behind the old mobile home, riding in the dirt until he got to the old, weed-filled gravel driveway.

With the small, no-headlight motorcycle geared into neutral and the engine killed, Paul silently zoomed the little TW 200 into his own suburban driveway. He then unlocked, and tugged upward on the garage door. He then walked the bike inside the dark garage.

After he closed the garage door, he used his green LED key chain light to find the interior door doorknob, and unlocked it. The interior storage room/light lock off of the garage was just as pitch-black, as usual. He closed the door to the garage behind him, before opening that room's door to the dining room, which was lit with some candles, in their glass enclosures. Emily was standing there, lighting a third one.

"Hi sweetie, I'm home," Paul said in a sing-song voice, as if he were a character in an old TV sitcom, coming home from a day at the job.

Emily walked over to him, and they hugged.
"Thank goodness your home."
"I always make it home, sweetie."

* * *

It was around 2:00 AM in the morning. Paul was awake, sitting in the living room, running his security shift. Emily was asleep. Paul was having his "lunch" of a couple of baked Yukon Gold potatoes from their garden. For his potatoes there was Red Feather-brand canned cheese and canned butter and all real, thanks to that particular New Zealand canned food manufacturer. He was thinking about the events on his way home, roughly two weeks earlier. With some instant coffee in-hand he was thinking about the good time he had had meeting Bill for the first time. A few days later, Paul had even donated to Bill that bag of dry dog food that he had recovered from the neighbor's house. He was really concerned about Bill, security-wise. It was only him and Miss Texaco, after all. Stealthy living seemed to be his main asset.

"ALERT ZONE ONE. ALERT ZONE ONE," the female voice of the Dakota Alert said through the MURS base station on Paul's desk, back in his study. That was the sensor on the north side of the house.

BOOM! One of his .12 gauge devices went off, on that same side of the house.

Paul ran into his almost pitch-black study, save for the gray light from the six-inch LOREX monitor. He grabbed his plate carrier, lifting it above his head and dropping it on his shoulders, securing it at each side of his waist. He donned his Kevlar helmet, securing its four-point chinstrap. He then attached his PVS-14 monocular to the mount at the front of the helmet, its J-arm placing it in front of his left eye. He then peeked through the closed mini-blinds towards the intersection and saw what looked like about twenty people, 70 yards-out, heading directly towards the house.

With the LOREX camera operating in gray-scale, IR-illuminated night vision mode, Paul saw someone on the monitor, running towards where someone had just tripped the .12 gauge booby trap, inside of the tangle-foot. Paul could hear his heart beating, loudly.

Paul grabbed the Benelli M2, putting the corded earplugs that were looped around its barrel behind his head, and into his ears. He then finger-loaded a loose cartridge into the shotgun's chamber. Paul released the bolt onto the chambered round, the Benelli making it's own intimidating ka-shlunk sound, although no one outside could hear it. The magazine tube was already filled with two-and-three-quarter .00 buckshot.

The main group had just rounded the corner of the intersection, off of the northeast corner of the house, and were now running towards the front of it. They had a variety of weapons: Baseball bats, machetes, two-or-three with pistols, and some rifles, ranging from old wooden-stocked bolt actions, to a couple of M4 rifles.

"ALERT ZONE ONE. ALERT ZONE ONE," the Dakota Alert base station repeated, as people continued to break the 20 yard-long, passive IR beam.

"ALERT ZONE TWO. ALERT ZONE TWO." That was the Dakota sensor just outside the south side of the property, aimed at the creek bed there.

Shit, Paul said, under his breath. In the darkness of his study, he quietly unlocked the window and slid it open.

BAM! A man's scream followed, again from the north side of the house. They had to be trying to negotiate the barbed wire tangle-foot, Paul thought. Some people in the street began firing into the garage, where they thought they heard the shots come from, and along the north-side of the house.

With that, Paul threw the rest of the window open, and began sweeping the group, from left-to-right through the red electronic cross-hair of the automatic shotgun's reflex sight: BOOM BOOM BOOM BOOM BOOM BOOM, the semi-automatic 12-gauge kicking like a mule. He dropped the Benelli on the floor. No time to reload it. He heard some male and female screams. He grabbed his M4, running for the bedroom, directly across the small hallway. A handful of incoming bullets began shattering the large rectangular window of Paul's study, some ricocheting off the partial brickwork, and some through the wall itself, below the window. Paul thought he felt something hit the back of his plate carrier.

"I'll kill you, you motherfucker," a wounded man on the street yelled.

"Let's get out of here," a dying woman screamed, laying near him in the darkness.

Emily was sitting up in bed. "What's going on," she asked, loudly.

"Get down! We're under attack! Grab your rifle and plate carrier," Paul yelled as he came to her side of the bed. As Paul pulled open the mini-blinds in their bedroom he saw a couple of men using the neighbor's shorter, four-foot cyclone fence about 30 feet away, trying to climb over their six-foot wooden fence into the blackberry-filled corner of their backyard. As the first attacker hopped-down into the five-foot tall blackberry hedgerow -

BAM! Then another man's scream. Another .12 gauge device set-off. The second person hopped back down off of the fence, out of view. Paul unlocked and slammed-open the window, rapidly firing semi-auto rounds out of his M4, putting them into the whole corner area of the property, along with a couple of extra rounds into the area where he thought the first guy had landed.

"Stay here! You see anyone out there, waste them!"

"Let me get my flashlight -"

"No! Don't turn that on! Use one of our green LED's!" Hunched over, Paul then ran back into his study, running directly into a man who had just entered his study through the open window. The muzzle of Paul's rifle was already sticking into the man's abdomen.

BAM BAM BAM BAM BAM. Paul fell backwards, as the heavy-set man fell forward, a bunch of 5.45 mm Russian bullets having exited his back.

"PAUL!"

"I'm OK," Pushing the body off of him, Paul then scrambled for his window, searching for targets. He saw nothing, other than several bodies lying in the street. He then closed and locked what was left of the bullet-shattered window.

Paul then ran down the hallway to check-out the rest of the house.

He ran to the other end of the house through the dining room, opening the door to the laundry/storage/light-lock room, then unlocking the exterior door there, to the backyard. Paul scanned the backyard through his night vision monocular. Hopefully, this mediocre group of refugees would already be leaving, based on what they just encountered. Paul also knew that *hope* was a four-letter word, however.

Paul stepped into the backyard, turning right, heading towards the north-side locked gate. As he got to the gate, kneeling, he scanned the area behind him, then reached-up from his crouch with his keys, quietly unlocking the padlocked gate.

As Paul began opening the gate a crack, he saw a male figure, laying face-down in the middle of the barbed wire tanglefoot. Behind the body were two men slowly coming towards Paul, trying to negotiate the barbed-wire, trying to step-over it here, stoop under it there. Paul shot one round at each of the three figures, using his unaided eye, behind the rifle's tubular red-dot sight. Paul was suddenly surprised by the technology he was using. The best-of-each-eye effect allowed him to see the red dot, placed on the target, as if it were being seen through the light-green view of the night vision monocular, itself. The fact that his red dot sight was already night vision compatible, with the weapons mount for the PVS-14 directly behind it on his rifle was just icing on the cake. Paul then back-tracked, running back along the exterior wall of the house.

"Emily, don't shoot! It's me coming towards the window" Paul yelled while running hunched, below the bedroom window frame.

"OK!"

Standing on an old molded-plastic chair, Paul looked over their south-side backyard fence. He saw a body on the ground, in the creek bed. He turned towards their bedroom window.

"Emily, are you OK" he asked her, before leaping down from the chair.

"I'm OK."

"Keep an eye on the inside of the house. It looks all clear out here. Just stay put."

"OK."

Quickly, Paul ran back towards the north-side of the backyard. Looking again through the backyard gate, past the tangle-foot, he saw people leaving the way they had come, heading east. A couple were running, others walking, or limping away, about 150 yards down the street from the intersection that his house sat next-to.

Paul had an idea. From a kneeling position, he turned-on the invisible-beam laser, mounted on the side of his M4 rifle. Looking over the top of his rifle through his helmet-mounted night vision monocular, Paul put the otherwise invisible dot onto individual targets, and started squeezing the trigger.

Stupid fucks, Paul was thinking as he dropped a third violent refugee, through the bright green world of his night vision device. He then got up, heading back to the other end of the back yard, along the outside wall of the house.

"Emily, it's me again, Paul. I'm heading to the window," Paul yelled as he approached their still-open bedroom window.
"Emily, it's me, Paul. Don't shoot. Do you hear me?"
"Yeah, I hear you."

Paul then looked at her through the open window. "Stay here and keep an eye out." Still in the backyard, Paul headed back to the south-side backyard gate, unlocking the padlock there. Opening the wooden gate just a crack, he scanned the street in front of the house, seeing nothing but several bodies, one of them moving. Paul went back down into the prone position. He opened the gate a little more, high-crawling through it, cradling his rifle as he crawled through the tall grass in his front yard,. Paul crawled right up to the cover of their large birch tree. He waited there, scanning the perimeter. With body armor and all Paul did a combat roll to the left, then got up, just in case they left a shooter behind. Walking towards where the wounded person lay, Paul continued scanning the area through his night vision. He didn't see anyone else.

It was a young woman, teenage-to-early twenties, an acne-scarred face; flabby body. She must have quickly lost weight, in all of this.

She was moaning in pain. Lying next to her was a children's-size baseball bat. Paul knelt-down next to her. "Is this what you were going to use on us, honey," Paul asked her as he picked-up the small wooden bat.

"I'm sorry... I just want to go home," she said, pitifully. She had taken some .00 buckshot in the upper legs, and abdomen.

"Where are you from?"

"The Plaza apartment complex... down the road."

"OK, yeah, I'll take you home." He was already thinking of a plan.

"Please... don't hurt me."

"Don't worry honey, I'll take you home." Paul then walked back to the house. However, he wasn't thinking of doing anything else for her.

Paul unlocked, then entered through the front door. "Emily, we're all clear. They're gone," he yelled to her. When Paul entered their bedroom, she was still looking out of the window, at an angle, the way he had shown her. She simply looked at him, shaking slightly, still scared.

"It's OK sweetie. they all left. None of the sensors are hitting on anything."

"Oh thank goodness."

"One of them is still alive, out in the street. Some girl. I told her I'd take her back to her apartment complex. I want to find-out exactly where this group of assholes came from."

"You're going to leave the house?"

"In about an hour. I want to give these dirtbags a chance to get home, if there's any left. Don't worry. We'll stay in radio contact."

"OK."

"Also, I just realized something: I need you to keep an eye-out on the wounded girl out there. I don't want her getting-up, and leaving on us."

"Oh my God, shouldn't we go out there and help her?"

"She was with a group of people that wanted to kill us and take everything we have. I don't think so. In case you're wondering, she had a small baseball bat on her. That's what she was 'gonna use on us. I'll need you on security."

"OK."

* * *

"To protect the sheep you got to catch the wolf and it takes a wolf to catch a wolf. You understand that?"
"What?"
"I said you protect the sheep by killing the motherfucking wolf!"

— Alonzo (played by Denzel Washington), from the film *Training Day* (2001).

After dragging the dead body out of his study Paul had spent the next 45 minutes prepping for his next mission. He didn't like the idea of using his small Nissan pickup, already loaded with bugout supplies, so he took the time to unload the contents from the bed of the truck to a spot just several feet away, back into their storage/light lock room. Paul was still wearing his OD green plate carrier and Kevlar helmet with night vision still attached, along with an OD/woodland pattern tactical vest now draped over the body armor. He traded his 5.45mm M4 to Emily for her CAR-15 and switched his magazines to all 5.56mm. Three of the magazines were marked TRACER.

While he was planning the remaining pre-dawn hours, he thought about any women and children who might be living where these attackers came from. Some of the people who attacked here tonight were women. Paul didn't want to hurt anybody who didn't have it coming to them, but in this new world, it was going to have to be total war, if he and Emily were going to survive.

Paul then opened the two-car garage door using his remote, the electronic garage door opener plugged-in to the PowerHub 1800 battery bank. He drove forward, out of the garage, bumping over a couple of bodies in the street. Oh well. Paul almost laughed to himself. He needed his dark side to stay turned-on at this moment. He brought the small truck's passenger side right-next to the wounded woman, in the middle of the street. He then got out, lifting her under the arms. A shrill scream followed.

"Shut the fuck up, Honey. You're the one attacking people's houses." Paul worked her into the front passenger seat, which was covered with an old shower curtain from Paul's painting supplies. He then threw her legs into the cab, slamming the door.

They drove east in the direction of the apartment complex, tactically blacked-out: No headlights or brake lights. Just Paul's helmet-mounted night vision monocular. After about one-half mile, Paul looked at her.

"Are you awake? I need you to stay awake. Are we heading in the right direction?"

"Yeah" she replied, closing her eyes. If she was worried about giving away her group, it was overwhelmed by her own personal instinct for survival.

Paul then got on his MURS hand-held. "Kathy, this is Paul. Radio check, over." He forgot to use a call sign.

"Hi Paul, I'm here."

"OK, out here," Paul said into the radio. "Don't we turn somewhere around here?" he then asked the girl.

"Left."

"OK."

They drove in front of an apartment complex, built in recent years to minimal code requirements. Typical of the low-cost housing that had been dominating southwest Washington.

"Which one of these blocks are you from?"

"Over there," she said, pointing with her left index finger to the right-side of the street. Paul stopped the truck. To the right, he saw an apartment block that had barbed wire strung in front of the main entrance to the building. It looked like someone here knew what they were doing and were organizing the people within this block of apartments.

Paul reached across, and opened the passenger door.

"Out you go, honey."

"I can't move," she said weakly.

Shutting-off the ignition and removing the key, Paul got out, went around to the passenger-side, and grabbed her bloody body by the arms, dumping her on the sidewalk. As her head hit the sidewalk, she became unconscious. He carefully folded-up the bloody old shower curtain, dumping it on the sidewalk as well. Paul shut the passenger-side door, went around the front of the small truck, then got back in. Turning the truck to the left, he looked for at least 100 yards of straight-line distance to the front of this specific block, within the apartment complex. He settled on the large parking lot surrounding a church, across the street from the apartments. Still inside the truck, Paul checked the range with a laser range-finder. Placing it in front of his night vision monocular, the LCD display read 167 yards. This should work. He then managed to drive the truck a little farther back, to a chain-link fence that marked the edge of that property.

Paul got out of the truck, mounting a small bi-pod to the rail under the front of his rifle. He then reached into his vest for a full 30-round magazine labeled TRACER, locking it into the rifle. Working the charging handle, Paul then leaned over the hood of his truck, placing the bi-pod mounted rifle there. Using the truck's engine as cover, and after making adjustments to the night vision monocular's electronic gain and focus, he began pumping tracer rounds into the bottom floor of the entire apartment building. BOOM BOOM BOOM BOOM. Even at this minimal range, his rounds resembled a scene from a Star Wars movie, with small bolts of light coming from his weapon. The rounds ended-up in various places, to include the insides of walls, floors, etc. some went completely through the building. Still burning with chemical material, most of the rounds began starting small, intensely-burning fires. Paul had put at least 20-rounds into the bottom of the building.

Paul realized something: These people would just set-up in one of the other adjacent apartment blocks, anyway. May as well do some urban renewal. He began firing into the other apartment buildings. When the magazine ran out, he dropped it with his trigger finger and reloaded another 30-round tracer magazine, putting more rounds into the entire apartment complex.

BAM.... BAM BAM. Paul heard a bullets hitting his truck. Damn. Not holes in my truck, too! He had bought the truck in the 1990's, brand-new, and had babied it ever since. It was as if rounds were hitting his own child. More incoming rounds were hitting the truck, one shattering the passenger-side window. Other rounds were whizzing in the air, past both ends of the truck.

"These motherfuckers," Paul said to himself. Through his bright-green world, he saw a person shooting from a third-story window. Shit! A scoped rifle -

BAM!

Paul was knocked backward, as a round went through the top of the hood and left fender, deflecting upward slightly, and hitting him smack in the upper middle portion of his plate carrier. He fell flat on his back, with his rifle flying into the air, landing somewhere behind him. Bullet spall hit underneath his chin, blood starting to run down his neck. Jesus, that was a big round, he thought. He felt as if someone had just hit the front of his plate carrier with a baseball bat, swung with all their force.

"Fuck," he said aloud, more pissed about his rifle hitting the pavement, than anything else. He almost started to laugh, though. He was actually enjoying this, the chaos of combat giving him a giddy sensation. Paul wondered what type of large caliber round he had just been hit with. He then rolled to his right, and began military high-crawling behind where he fell, looking for his rifle. Once he found it several yards away, he then cradled the rifle inside of his elbows, thinking of where to re-position himself.

"Alright." He didn't have any other cover out here. He turned around, high-crawling back to the rear driver-side wheel on the small truck, supporting the rifle on the small rear step-bumper this time, taking aim at the more-elevated target. He aimed just below the window, itself. BAM BAM BAM, more tracers that will soon start setting that upper portion of the building on fire.

Shit. No one there, Paul noticed. The shooter changed position, just like he would have done. Damn, OK. Maybe it was time to get out of here, Paul thought. He then let loose with his last 20 rounds of 5.56 mm tracer at the first floor of a third apartment building. He did a complete combat roll of his body, back behind the cover of the rear wheel. He then got back into the small white truck, starting the engine, hauling ass out of there, rounds still hitting the truck.

As he headed home, he looked to the left. The girl he had dropped onto the sidewalk was still lying there.

* * *

As Paul arrived home he could now see a red glow from the direction of the apartments. In this new world of no electrical grid, it was now easy to notice such things at distance, without the usual light pollution.

At the house itself, bullet holes and bodies were everywhere. Paul drove over a couple of them as he remotely opened the garage door, backing into the dark garage.

Paul killed the truck's engine, then closed the garage door. Once again, he was in complete darkness. Turning off the night vision monocular, he then used the green LED light on his keychain to light his way between the two backed-in trucks, to the house door.

The laundry/storage room off of the garage was dark, as usual. Paul continued using the green LED light, until he reached the next door to the dining room, just a few feet away.

Emily was standing there in the dining room, in the light of lit candles, still wearing her coyote-colored Condor-brand plate carrier and Kevlar helmet, with BDU cover.
"Oh my God, you're covered in blood."
"I am?"
"Yes! You've been shot!"
"Oh, a round hit my plate carrier, and some of the stuff hit me under my chin."
"Let me get the first-aid kit."

* * *

Paul had just been able to stay awake while Emily tended to his injuries from the bullet spall. Later, around sunrise Paul thought he would give them both a treat. He hooked-up both the coffee maker and the bean grinder to the Powerhub 1800, and brewed some well-earned, fresh Starbucks. He was taking a break, while Emily went back to bed.

The bodies. They were everywhere in front of the house, the north side of the house, and down the street to the east, where the house faced, on the intersection. At least 12, that he could count, in addition to the one he had to drag out of his study, out the front door, earlier that morning.

What do I do? Bury them, Paul asked himself, as he looked out of their living room window, coffee in hand. Too much physical effort. He and Emily both needed to watch their caloric output, as well as input, until they knew that their food situation was more secure.

Burn them? Yeah, that was possible. They had the fuel. But that would draw people with the smoke. At night? The flames would draw people as well. Jesus. Paul just couldn't think of anything. If he were to burn them, it would have to be away from the house...

Paul thought some more... Wait... That's it! I'll load the bodies into the Nissan and take them somewhere else, *then* burn them. He also needed to assess the damage to the truck, since it was now ridden with bullet holes. Emily came into the living room, dark circles under her eyes after sleeping only a couple of hours after the early AM ordeal.

"Paul, we need to get out of here."

"Yeah, but we won the fight, for now."

"But whoever you didn't already kill will come back here and attack us."

"I think I removed most of the competition. Besides, I don't think they have a home around here, anymore."

"What do mean?"

"I used tracers to burn-down all the apartments, where they lived."

"My gosh... But what if a larger group attacks us next time?"

"Yeah... You're right. In the meantime, I need to deal with these bodies."

Paul downed a small, 30 grams of protein container of *Premier Protein* then set about assessing the damage to his small, white Nissan pickup. The passenger-side window was shattered from a single bullet hole. There were numerous bullet holes in the passenger-side of the cab-high fiberglass canopy and along the entire body length, on that side.

With his rifle slung across his back, muzzle facing down and a pair of leather work gloves, Paul went about picking-up the bodies. Although it was rough handling the bodies by himself, he didn't feel that he should ask Emily to clean up his mess. She was traumatized enough, already. He let her go back to sleep. After laying a sheet of vapor barrier plastic in the bed of his truck for a second time, he shoved the bodies into the bed of his low-canopied Nissan. He would obviously need to make at least a second trip. As Paul shoved the last of the bodies for this first load into the truck's bed, he saw some neighbors to the north, about three-hundred yards away, at the end of a cull-de-sac, watching him.

As he started the truck, Paul continued thinking. Where can I put these bodies? An idea came to mind.

He drove towards a large open area, underneath some power lines, not far from the neighborhood. As he traveled down the dirt access road, he backed-up into some shrubs. He then began pulling the bodies out, dumping them into a pile. As he piled them on top of each other, he grabbed nearby dead vegetation, throwing it on top of each layer of the bodies. As he pulled-out an OD green jerry-can fuel container, he stopped to think for a moment: Why should I even bother to burn them? Wild animals will just start chewing on them, anyway. Why spoil it for them? At least they'll get something out of this.

Driving back to the house after unloading the second load, Paul then thought about disease. Even though it wasn't close to the house, the combination of food for wild dogs, and disease from these bodies just wasn't worth it. Back in 2008 there were so many abandoned dogs nationwide as a result of the financial collapse. He didn't even want to think of how many wild dogs were out here now.

After returning with the third load of bodies, pulling them out and adding them to the pile, Paul went ahead and started dousing the entire five-gallon container of stabilized gasoline onto the pile of corpses. After securing the empty fuel container, he pulled out a small book of matches, lighting just one-

Whoosh! Clothes, human skin, native shrubbery, grass and blackberry vines all began burning. Paul watched it for a moment, then got back into the small white pickup, and left.

As he drove the small, white bullet-riddled truck back home, Paul wondered how many more local people were willing to attack their house at this point. He had already created a pretty good body count which should give a pretty good warning, in itself.

When would a larger group of people take over the area? Maybe it *was* time to bug out. But where? How depopulated was the area, as of now? What threats from outside the area would now appear? It would require Paul to recon their area on a regular basis. He hated to think like a certain former Secretary of Defense, but the late Donald Rumsfeld's thinking applied here: What were the known knowns? The known unknowns? The unknown unknowns?

Snuffy

List of Acronyms

ABM: Anti-Ballistic Missile

ACU: Army Combat Uniform.

ALICE: All-Purpose Lightweight Individual Carrying Equipment. The US military's load bearing system for web gear and backpacks, developed in the early 1970's. Replaced by the more-modern MOLLE system.

AP: Armor Piercing.

API: Armor-Piercing Incendiary.

APT: Armor-Piercing Tracer.

AR15: The civilian version of the military-issue M16.

ASAP: As Soon As Possible.

BDU: Battle Dress Uniform. Worn by every branch of the U.S. Military, from the early 1980's to the late 2000's.

CAR-15: The original short-carbine version of the AR-15 rifle.

CADPAT: Canadian Disruption Pattern.

CFR: Council on Foreign Relations.

COG: Continuity of Government. The highly classified plan by the US Government to maintain governance in the event of a national emergency, when key leadership has been removed, in particular.

CONUS: Continental United States.

ECWS: Extreme Cold Weather System.

FMJ: Full Metal Jacket

HUMMWV: High Mobility Multipurpose Wheeled Vehicle.

IR: Infra-Red.

JB Weld: The common name brand for metal-filled epoxy. Its use is also referred to as "cold welding."

J-SOC: The U.S. Military's Joint Special Operations Command.

K-Pot: Kevlar helmet.

M2: 50 Cal. Browning Machinegun. Also known as Ma Deuce.

M4: The US military's current standard-issue M16/AR15-platform rifle, replacing the M16-A2. Similar to the Vietnam-era CAR-15 Colt Commando.

M16: The US military's original standard issue rifle in 5.56 mm NATO (.223 cal.), used since The Vietnam War.

MEPS: Military Examination and Processing Station. Formerly known as AFEES (Armed Forces Entrance and Examination Station), until 1982.

MOLLE: The U.S. military's current Modular Lightweight Load-carrying Equipment system (Pronounced "Molly"), which replaced the Vietnam-era ALICE system.

MRE: Meal, Ready-to-Eat. The U.S. military's current individual field ration, replacing the 1960's to early 1980's C-Ration meal.

OD: Olive drab.

OPSEC: Operational Security. Common military phrase, borrowed years ago by the survivalist community.

POV: Privately Owned Vehicle.

SATCOM: Satellite Communications

ABOUT THE AUTHOR

Joe Snuffy is the pen name of a retired U.S. Army (Reserve) Intelligence Officer, who served numerous state-side tours during the Iraq and Afghan occupations.

Snuffy worked everything from strategic counterintelligence (to include intercepting a former Taliban *within* the U.S.), to working strategic intelligence, briefing three-star corps commanders.

The author has dedicated himself to living and working as a professional survivalist. This decision was based on his own life experiences and extensive research, studying various works such as the 1972 MIT/Club of Rome *Limits to Growth* study, the writings of John Michael Greer, Dr. Jared Diamond, Dr. Joseph Tainter, Nicole Foss (a.k.a. *Stoneleigh* from The Automatic Earth website), Gail Tverberg, Alice Friedman and others.

57006265R00108

Made in the USA
Columbia, SC
04 May 2019